TELL ME AGAIN
HOW A CRUSH
SHOULD
FEEL

ALSO BY SARA FARIZAN

IF YOU COULD BE MINE

TELL ME AGAIN HOW A CRUSH SHOULD FEEL

SARA FARIZAN

ALGONQUIN   2015

Published by
Algonquin Young Readers
an imprint of Algonquin Books of Chapel Hill
Post Office Box 2225
Chapel Hill, North Carolina 27515-2225

a division of
Workman Publishing
225 Varick Street
New York, New York 10014

First paperback edition, Algonquin Young Readers, October 2015.
Originally published in hardcover by Algonquin Young Readers, October 2014.
Printed in the United States of America.
Design by Linda McCarthy.

Library of Congress Cataloging-in-Publication Data
Farizan, Sara.
    Tell me again how a crush should feel / Sara Farizan.
        pages cm
    Summary: High school junior Leila's Persian heritage already makes her
    different from her classmates at Armstead Academy, and if word got out
    that she liked girls life would be twice as hard, but when a new girl,
    Saskia, shows up, Leila starts to take risks she never thought she would,
    especially when it looks as if the attraction between them is mutual, so she
    struggles to sort out her growing feelings by confiding in her old friends.
    ISBN 978-1-61620-284-2 (HC)
    [1. Love—Fiction. 2. High schools—Fiction. 3. Schools—Fiction.
    4. Lesbians—Fiction. 5. Iranian Americans—Fiction. 6. Friendship—
    Fiction.] I. Title.
    PZ7.F179Te 2014
    [Fic]—dc23   2014021580

ISBN 978-1-61620-549-2 (PB)

10 9 8 7 6 5 4 3 2 1
First Paperback Edition

**For my Mr. Miyagi, Chris Lynch,
and my Fairy Godmother, Elise Howard.**
Thank you for believing in me, even when
I don't believe in myself sometimes.

ONE

My copy of *The Color Purple* lies in front of me on my desk, the spine bent and wrinkled from the many times I've pored over the book. I have so many things to say about the beautiful prose, the characters, but I won't . . . because I, Leila Azadi, am a Persian scaredy-cat. I can't believe even English class makes me anxious these days.

"Now, when Walker describes Shug through Celie's eyes, what is she trying to convey?" Ms. Taylor has, of course, managed to touch on the one subject in *The Color Purple* that I can't even begin to comment on.

Please don't call on me.

Please don't call on me.

Ms. Taylor is eyeing the class like a hawk about to

swoop down on some unsuspecting field mice. A really hot hawk with great hair and an appreciation for literature, I might add . . . which reminds me, I should stop crushing on her in class, especially since it's the beginning of the school year.

Ms. Taylor sets her sights on my friend Tess. "Any thoughts?" she asks.

Tess looks up at Ms. Taylor with those mousy eyes, her retainer glistening under the fluorescent lights. I've told her to stop wearing it at school, but she insists her teeth will not be compromised for popularity.

"I think Celie finds Shug attractive . . . like in a romantic fashion," Tess says.

The snickering begins with Ashley Martin and Lisa Katz. They're the girls every guy at our school has fantasized about since we were in ninth grade, which I find strangely disturbing. I'm pretty sure Mr. Harris, our science teacher, has been seeing Ashley outside of school. I should probably tell Ms. Taylor that because she and Mr. Harris have been dating since the beginning of the school year. They have never said anything about it, but it's so obvious, especially when he comes all the way from the science building to borrow chalk from her. I should get him a gift card to Staples and tell him about all the discounts he can get on office supplies.

Mr. Harris is like one of those guys who loved his time in high school and decided never to grow up. I would probably find him endearing and dreamy like everyone else if I didn't resent him for dating a woman far superior to him . . . and if I wasn't failing his snooze of a class. Why would I ever care about frictionless acceleration anyway? How is that ever going to get me a girlfriend?

Not that I dare think about that. I'm not ready to announce my lady-loving inclinations as yet. I can hear the whispering, knowing that what they are snickering about could easily be me. I'm already different enough at this school. I don't need to add anything else to that.

As Tess struggles through her answer to Ms. Taylor's question, Ashley cackles with the fervor and depth that only a bitchy blond sixteen-year-old can muster. Apparently Lisa is no longer interested. She looks back to her notebook, hiding her face by pulling her brown bangs down. It's a habit she's had since we were kids.

Lisa and I went to the same private elementary school. She's richer than God—her father is some kind of CEO—plus she's attractive and dresses well. Considering our totally different social circles now, it's hard to believe we were friends as kids. But back then we both had an obsession with Roald Dahl books, and that was all that was necessary.

"Very good, Tess," says Ms. Taylor. "Celie does have strong feelings for Shug. Is it possible for her, even though she is married, to be attracted to another woman?"

The class is silent again. I hate when this happens. I've never done well with awkward silences or pauses. I can always hear people breathing. I can hear *myself* breathe. It's the most uncomfortable feeling ever. Usually I'd make a joke or something, but this subject is too risky. They'd all know.

"Robert? What do you think?" Ms. Taylor has caught another of Armstead Academy's finest in her talons now. Robert Peters is on the soccer team, rows on the crew team, and gets great grades, but I don't understand why he works so hard. His parents own a potato chip brand popular in New England, and Robert will inherit the company when he grows up. He always has a Gatorade bottle with him, full of piss-yellow Gatorade and vodka. He gets a little loopy from the booze by history, which is two periods away, but keeps it together enough that teachers don't notice.

"I don't know, Ms. Taylor. I've never been married and I'm not a lesbian." Everyone laughs, this time including me. I don't really mean it, but the fake laugh is high school protocol. Everything's a lark when you're rich and handsome, like Robert. Why upset the status quo? Though I'm not one to talk. My dad's a surgeon.

My parents are both originally from Iran and think education is the most important thing. To give them credit, Armstead has facilities and resources beyond those of a lot of small colleges. We have a sleek fitness gym to train Olympic athletes (we've had two in the past eight years) and our dining hall is like a castle out of Harry Potter.

At first, when I came here in ninth grade, I really loved the place. I got along with everybody, I loved my classes, and I enjoyed sports. It all kind of went awry after meeting Anastasia this past summer at a Global Young Leaders of the Future camp, where we spent two weeks having mock debates while representing our countries in the United Nations. I was put in the Algeria group, the only Middle Eastern country other than Israel represented. Anastasia was representing Ghana, but she was from France.

Anastasia had a red birthmark near her eyebrow that she didn't seem at all self-conscious about. One day she cornered me in the dorm lounge and talked to me about the concept of privilege and how I was a naive, spoiled girl who didn't know anything about the world around me. I found her fascinating.

By the time the Festival of Nations came around, where we all dressed up in inappropriate ethnic garb from our represented countries, Anastasia came up to me while

I wore a hijab and she was wearing a dashiki, which was clearly meant for a man. We looked ridiculous, but we had been talking for days about our favorite musicians, her melodramatic poems, and my crap photography skills, and by this time there was this . . . *tension* between us. I had no idea what that tension was; I just knew I shouldn't pursue it. But I couldn't stop thinking about it, either.

Anastasia asked me to help her find her *djembe* drum in her dorm room before the festival got underway. We went upstairs to her room, and she locked the door. She swung me around by my arm and asked me if I had ever been properly kissed before. I thought back to playing spin the bottle in sixth grade and kissing Andrew Cassidy. His kiss tasted like Fritos, a snack I can't stand. Then there had been my semiformal date, Greg Crawford. We kissed for ten minutes. I wanted to feel something, but I didn't.

So here was Anastasia, gently tugging at my *hijab*-covered arm, breathing softly on my lips, looking at the shape of my eyebrows and pushing back my head scarf with her other hand. I told her that no, I didn't think I had been properly kissed. And then it happened.

She inched closer. My ears were warm enough to heat up a Hot Pocket. My stomach felt the way it had on the Thunderbolt coaster at Six Flags New England. I wondered if Anastasia would know that I practiced kissing on my pillow and could never quite figure out where my tongue was supposed to go.

All my wondering was put to rest when our lips met. The kiss started slow, her lips figuring me out, asking whether it was okay to continue their dance. I backed away slightly, looked her in the eye—and started to cry.

And then I knew for sure what I had been trying to avoid for so long. Everything rushed to the surface. I cried as I remembered throwing the dress I had received for my third birthday on the floor. I cried as I remembered wanting to be best friends with a girl in fifth grade because she was so pretty. I cried as I remembered always rescuing the girl, played by a stuffed animal, while pretending to be Indiana Jones. I cried and Anastasia kissed my lips again, this time aggressively, her tongue asking for acceptance. We missed the festival, but we couldn't have cared less.

Our fling lasted through a couple more make-out sessions, but Anastasia ended up liking some guy named Enrique by the time the mock United Nations summit rolled around at the end of the summer. I was heartbroken. I threatened almost every country at the conference with whatever military capabilities Algeria had. My other group members had to appease everyone afterward by offering to export more oil. After days of the two of us not speaking, the program came to an end and Anastasia pulled me aside in the girls' bathroom.

She said this was only the beginning for me and I was going to find someone special. She said she was a mess and I could do better. At the time I didn't believe her, but I was willing to put up with her melodrama for one last kiss. We broke apart when we heard a toilet flush. A Japanese girl came out of the stall, washed her hands, and booked it out of there.

After this past summer, I came back a little wiser to the universe, having met people from all over the world. I realized I was different, and that Anastasia might not have been the only one who had figured that out about me.

"Leila, what do you think?" Ms. Taylor's question pulls me out of my daydreams. I feel everyone's eyes on me.

What do I think? After the summer I was thinking too much. I started noticing things I hadn't before, like our hallway janitor, who had to clean up the snack wrappers we tossed onto the floor, even though a wastebasket was a few feet away. I started noticing how all the black kids in our grade, seven in total, sat in one spot by themselves and were always pointedly asked what they thought in class whenever we studied slavery or the civil rights movement.

Greg hates being asked, and I don't know why he doesn't say something to his mother, who is on the board of trustees.

I also began to notice how white everything was. The students, the students' teeth, and the fences surrounding the outdoor swimming pools we never used. We all seemed to categorize ourselves without ever explicitly saying anything. Where does that leave students who don't have a clear category?

"Can Celie be attracted to another woman?" Ms. Taylor is standing near my desk. Ashley Martin folds her arms and Robert Peters guzzles his Gatorade bottle.

"With a husband as awful as Celie's, I don't blame her. Am I right?" I say with a chuckle that almost sounds real amid the laughter of my peers.

TWO

"What are you up to?"

Greg pulls up a chair next to me in the computer lab. I quickly minimize Anastasia's Facebook page and turn to him. So maybe I'm not completely over her.

"Oh, nothing. What's up?"

"I saw the new trailer for *Zombie Killers Part V.* It's pretty sick."

"No way! The teaser trailer wasn't supposed to come out until November!"

"Hey, I know a guy. Here, I'll show you," he says, commandeering my computer as I shift my chair a little to the side.

Greg's the kind of guy I wish I could crush on. He and I have a lot in common. We both like comic books and hip-hop, and we both think that Naya Rivera is our dream girl—though he doesn't know that. He types in a web address and hovers the arrow over grainy footage of zombies parachuting out of the sky.

"Holy crap!" I say, and Greg turns to face me.

"I know!" We look at each other in excitement, but his eyes linger a little too long. I scoot away as he rubs the nape of his neck and looks back at the screen, almost as an apology.

At the semiformal dance we went to last year, he told me he'd liked me for a long time. I care about Greg . . . I just wish he didn't have a crush on me. I suppose it's flattering and makes me feel pretty. Other people have told me the same thing, but I never feel that way. I feel . . . not yet assembled, if that even makes sense.

After our make-out session last spring, I didn't call Greg for about two weeks. Eventually he called and asked if I was okay. I told him I didn't want to ruin our friendship by dating, and I could tell he was upset, but he agreed that our friendship was more important. I knew he'd be fine and date some hot girl who would treat him like crap, and I'd be left to moon over some girl of my own.

"I thought McNair died in the last one," I say, watching the trailer on the screen.

"Well, he came back as a zombie."

"But he's a zombie hunter. So he's hunting his own kind? Talk about self-loathing." God, nothing in this franchise makes sense. When women in bikinis who have nothing to do with the plot show up, Greg clears his throat. I pretend I don't notice and hope I'm not blushing.

I haven't had a crush on anyone from school, which is a blessing. At Armstead everyone knows everything about everyone, even people you've never had a conversation with. While the school is physically impressive and has a lot of land and buildings, there are less than six hundred students, grades seven through twelve, inhabiting its halls. There are paintings and photographs of former educators and students, most of which look to be of the WASP variety, dating from the school's inception in the 1800s.

The campus boasts several athletic fields, a giant gymnasium, a hockey rink, tennis courts, squash courts, a performing arts center, a photography lab, a science building, a building for the middle school, and three computer labs. There's also a library, which is small and mostly used as a place to nap or read magazines.

The *Zombie Killers* trailer ends and Greg moves to a chair next to mine. "Are you going to Lisa Katz's party this weekend?" he asks, checking his Facebook newsfeed.

"I didn't know I was invited." Greg and I aren't exactly in the cool group. We're more in the middle—not popular but not ostracized, either. There are a few well-established tiers within the social hierarchy at Armstead, yet Greg and I have somehow managed to remain floaters.

The cool kids are Ashley, Lisa, and their shopping buddies, some jocks, and some billionaire kids. I don't understand how cool kids find one another. It's like they have sonar for who is socially acceptable and who isn't.

"Yeah, it's like a back-to-school thing," Greg says. "Almost everyone's invited. You going?"

"Oh, I don't know. I have a ton of work."

"Homework? It's a Lisa Katz party, Leila! I've heard her house is badass. We've got to check it out!"

I don't tell Greg that I went to Lisa's house all the time when I was younger. She and I always had a pretty good time, until her mother showed up. Stephanie Katz always put me on edge. There was something about her that made me nervous all the time. She didn't yell or scream. She would just phrase things in a certain way that made you feel inferior or useless, like "I didn't think you were familiar with Charles Dickens's work," or "Your mother has such an interesting accent. The way she says '*vatermelon*' instead of 'watermelon.'"

Lisa and I stopped hanging out when she came to

Armstead in seventh grade. I came in ninth grade, and Lisa wasn't superenthused to see me in her class. By the time I got here from my old school, Ashley had kind of swooped in on Lisa. They had this weird bond that I didn't understand. They talked about clothes and TV shows I never had an interest in. It was like watching a *Seventeen* magazine article come to life, where the models look like they're laughing about something you just wouldn't understand. I think I had a window to join in but blew it when Ashley looked down and saw I was wearing sandals with socks. I have since remedied this, but in my defense it was cold and those sandals were within Armstead dress code. I don't think Lisa or I really missed each other that much, but sometimes I wonder how she's doing when I see her in class. She seems so . . . *different* now.

Lisa's older brother, Steve, died last year in a car accident on Route 128. Back when we were younger, Steve would hang out with me and show me his X-Men action figures when his sister had to practice the piano. Lisa hated playing, but her mother insisted it was a skill she would be thankful for in the future, and she had to practice every day at 5:15. I heard "Für Elise" over and over again while Colossus and Sabretooth duked it out for supremacy. Sometimes Steve let me, as Colossus, win.

During Steve's funeral service, Lisa sat quietly next to her mom, pulling down her bangs in front of her eyes. For the shivah, a few days later, I went over to her house with a plastic bag in my hand. Ashley and all the popular kids were leaving as I walked in. We said hey, and they pointed me in Lisa's direction. I stood around for a while, feeling a little out of place. I hadn't been to her house in ages. The house seemed twice as big as I remembered and so empty, even with all the mourners ignoring the table full of food. Lisa made eye contact with me and excused herself from a group of her father's business partners.

"Thanks for coming." Lisa said.

We hadn't really spoken outside of school for so long—it was funny talking to someone I didn't really know anymore in a setting that no longer seemed familiar, either.

"It was a nice service the other day."

She nodded.

"I'm sorry. I know you've probably been hearing a lot of that for the past week, but . . . I'm really sorry. Steve was a good guy."

"He was. A really good guy."

She looked away from me. Not at anything or anyone in particular, just away from me.

"Do you still play piano?"

She looked at me like I had just asked her an intimate question about her sex life. But whatever surprise she felt at the question was soon masked again with indifference.

"Yeah. I still play."

"Practice at five fifteen?" I asked.

She made a noise that sounded like a cough, though given the circumstances I think that was the best version of a laugh she could muster.

"Not so much anymore, what with soccer and everything."

I nodded.

"He'd always play video games with me when you'd go off to practice. He didn't have to, but I always thought he was so cool, being older and everything. I always wished I had a big brother like him."

She nodded politely, looking away from me again.

"I told him that once. I think I was about eight. He smiled and gave me this."

I pulled a Colossus action figure from the plastic bag and gave it to Lisa.

"I thought you might want to have it back. I know it's lame—"

She hugged me. I almost jumped back in shock.

"Thank you."

We released and I gave her a small smile.

"Anyway, I better let you get back to things. Listen, I know, we're not best friends or whatever, but if you need anything—" I thought I saw a hint of a smile, but I wasn't sure. I walked away as quickly as I could. I didn't want to be there anymore.

"Damn. Lisa's e-vite has a hundred RSVPs," Greg says, pulling me back to the present and the computer lab. He's scrolling down the guest list, his eyes getting wider as the list goes on and on.

When is that stupid bell going to ring?

THREE

I really can't stand soccer. Armstead requires that all students participate in some sort of after-school activity, most of which are sports. I'm on the thirds team, which is a tier below junior varsity, basically designed for all the scrawny, fat, or uncoordinated players who don't have anywhere else to go.

Last season I faked an injury to my ankle that kept me on the sideline for about two weeks. It was pretty amazing. This year I've been working on trying to fake ulcers by reading the symptoms online and practicing in the mirror. It's going to be my ailment of the season. I always have to keep things fresh and believable.

Sometimes our coach will have us run for half an hour,

mostly because he doesn't know what else to do with us. Some girls take it seriously, wanting to make JV next season so they can prove to their parents that they are athletic and to themselves that they are worthy to grace the Armstead fields with their presence. I don't kid myself.

On these half-hour runs, I usually slip away and hide in the basement of our cafeteria, sometimes alone, sometimes with Tess. When it's about time to go back to practice, we jog in place for a good two minutes and then head back down the hill to the field.

Today, Coach has insisted that we run for forty-five minutes, giving me and Tess plenty of time to chat.

"Basement?" I whisper to her as we begin to run with the rest of the team.

"I don't know, Leila. I kind of feel like running today."

"Are you kidding me? Why do you want to kill yourself for no reason?"

"It's not for no reason. Running can be an enjoyable experience."

I look at her in bewilderment. I have never understood that whole notion of getting a "runner's high" or becoming "addicted" to exercise. My mother is a big believer in both those things. She's convinced that if I go to the gym with her, I'll suddenly fall in love with the idea of running on treadmills and sweating all over hip abductor machines while La Bouche's "Be My Lover" plays over and over. I'm on the curvy side, which has somehow become a crime. I am happy with my appearance, thank you very much. My older sister, Nahal, however, has always been skinny, which gets on my nerves, especially when she and my mom swap clothes and talk about the new sale at Bloomingdale's.

I finally coax Tess into joining me in the basement, and we sit down on a granite ledge. We've been friends since we both started at Armstead in ninth grade, mostly because she's one of the only people at this school with a sense of humor and because we're in the same Japanese class. Sometimes she references things I don't understand because she's so much smarter than me and everyone else, but she never makes me feel bad about it. I think what makes us work is that neither one of us understands things teenage girls are supposed to be interested in. Tess would rather read about new discoveries in the world of synthetic skin than know everything about pop stars. I make her laugh in assembly and sometimes cheat off her during Japanese quizzes. I would feel bad about it if the quizzes didn't count for 1 percent of our final grade.

Tess works hard at school and her dad is an English teacher at Armstead as well as the junior class adviser. She is kind of embarrassed about being a "faculty brat," and I think she feels like she always has to prove that she belongs here on her own merits, though I want to tell her that nobody really *belongs* here unless your name is on a building or you came over on the *Mayflower*.

"Okay, Tess, what's with this running thing? You really want to? Voluntarily?"

"I want to get in shape for squash season. It's coming up, and I might actually have a chance at making the team this year."

"Squash season isn't for another four months!"

"Maybe I want to try and be good at soccer, too."

Fair enough. Who am I to begrudge her soccer happiness? If she is a masochist, so be it.

"Leila, if you hate soccer so much, why don't you do something else?"

"Like what? Outdoors club? Hike a mountain and get eaten by a cougar or choke to death on granola?" Tess pretends to play a tiny violin.

"Maybe you should audition for the play. You are kind of dramatic sometimes."

"God, and be a theater kid? They all take themselves so seriously."

"What's wrong with that?"

That shuts me up. I hate when she's right. Which is usually always.

"Lisa Katz is having a party this Friday," I say. "Greg wants to go and is trying to convince me."

"That's nice," Tess says, looking away to trace the veins in the granite wall with her finger. Tess wouldn't speak to me for a while after I told her Greg and I made out, even though I explained that we had decided to remain friends. She's had a crush on him for forever but will never do anything about it.

"Do you want to come with us?"

"I don't want to be a third wheel," Tess says.

I moan. "It's not a date!" It astounds me that Tess is as brilliant as she is and still hasn't figured out I'm gay. I wish there was a manual on how to come out and what a young gay person is supposed to do. Like, is there a secret handshake I don't know about?

"I have a ton of homework anyway. Besides Ms. Taylor's coming over for dinner on Thursday and that's going to use up my whole night."

"Really? That sounds cool."

Invite me over!

Invite me over!

"It does? Mom and I are just going to sit there and

have to listen to my dad and Ms. Taylor go on and on about Toni Morrison. Should be oodles of fun."

It *would* be oodles of fun! I love Ms. Taylor's enthusiasm for literature. And the way she flips her hair when she reads a passage. And that she sometimes has a button undone on her sweater that shouldn't be. God, I hate hormones.

"I wouldn't mind hearing her musings on Morrison…," I suggest with my eyebrows comically raised.

"Seriously? Well, if you have nothing else to do, we'd love to have you over." *Tess, I think I'm trying to tell you something.* If the idea that I'm gay is so beyond the realm of possibility for someone as smart and sensitive as Tess, what would everyone else at Armstead make of this information?

"Sounds like a plan. Thanks." I check the clock on the wall. "It's time." We stand up and begin to run in place.

"Dad says there's a new student coming into our grade this week," Tess says.

"But we've been in school for two weeks already."

"Her family's just moved here from Indonesia or Dubai or someplace. Dad's probably going to make me show her around. I hate when he does that, because it eats up all my study halls."

"I'll do it. I hate study hall."

"Cool. Thanks."

In two minutes I'm panting and heaving, and Tess hasn't even broken a sweat. She quits running in place and walks over to the water fountain to dab water under her armpits and a little at the collar of her T-shirt. Fake sweat. I've taught her well.

Back at practice, Coach has us partner up and work on kicking the ball to one another. The girls' varsity team is in the middle of practice at the nicer field nearby. Ashley Martin's long legs look like they could break me in half as she kicks the ball halfway down the field. When she plays soccer, her true nature comes out. She becomes a fierce, wild, and feral beast who will stop at nothing to get her way. Ashley kicks the ball to Lisa, who receives it effortlessly and continues down the field. I was in awe of how easily soccer came to Lisa when we were kids; she hasn't lost it.

"Leila! Pass the ball!" Tess shouts.

I pass the ball, then look back toward the varsity practice to see Lisa sidestepping her opponent and dribbling farther down the field. It's so easy for her, it doesn't look like she's even trying; she's just going through the motions. She shoots and scores, wiping her face with her shirt while receiving pats on the back from her teammates.

"Leila, look out!" The ball clocks me in the boobs.

"SHIT, TESS!"

I wrap my arms around my chest and crouch down. My eyes are tearing up a little.

I really can't stand soccer.

FOUR

Dad picks me up after school. I have two more months until I get my license, but until then I have to rely on him for rides, which means listening to Bob Edwards and *The World* on PRI and to Dad's complaining about the NASDAQ report.

"Your sister is having dinner with us tonight," he says, smiling. He loves it when Nahal comes over, and especially loves that she's going to be a doctor just like him. She goes to Harvard, so she's close by and comes over *all* the time. Nahal's twenty-one—you'd think she'd be barhopping and cutting loose a little bit on the weekends, or at least having dinner parties or something with her lame pre-med friends. Though any sort of social life would interfere with her rubbing how perfect she is in my face.

"Again? Doesn't she have things to do at school or something?"

"She's studying hard. You should learn from her." The NASDAQ report comes on. Stocks are down again.

"How I miss the late nineties," Dad says.

Dad has these bouts of nostalgia when he realizes he's losing money. Tax time, reviewing Mom's credit card statement, paying tuition bills—he just starts reminiscing with no one in particular and gets this over-the-top dreamy look in his eye. I ask if I can turn the radio station and he concedes. We listen to hip-hop for about four minutes.

"Leila, what is this we're listening to? All this talk about butts! You listen to this garbage?"

"Yes, I do, Dad."

He pops in one of his Iranian CDs. Jeez. It's from the eighties and I'm pretty sure the guy singing is well past dead. He sings about losing his love, which I'm convinced all Iranian songs are about. We're really into loss, depression, and martyrdom, except at parties where we dance and discuss whose kid is graduating cum laude from Princeton or who just had a baby. Dad rolls his window down and turns up the volume, yelling the song in Farsi on Route 128, trying to make me laugh but really just making me embarrassed. He laughs after a while and rolls the window up.

"Okay, enough torture. You can listen to your butt songs."

Nahal is making Dad salivate, asking him questions about organic chemistry for her homework while I play video games online. I see the two of them engaged in what Nahal is studying, and it's not in me to get jealous anymore. I know they get along because they're practically the same person. They both read biographies, they're both very traditional, and they love academia and science. I think they look at me like a physics equation they can't solve.

Mom comes over with a plate of fruit. "Are you doing your homework, Leila?"

I minimize the video game window and pull up an essay I wrote last semester.

"Yup. On page two."

"I got a call from Mr. Harris. He's concerned about your last quiz."

"Don't worry, Mom. I'll do better on the next one."

"Do you want me to hire a science tutor for you?" I've had math tutors since I was in fourth grade. One was a single mother of two in her forties who taught in public school. She fed me Goldfish crackers. Another was a Harvard graduate student majoring in Japanese. He fed me wasabi peas and

Pocky. My favorite was a blind, elderly Iranian guy who smoked while I typed numbers into his robotic talking calculator. He gave me Kit Kats and Coca-Cola. With tutors I basically eat their food, understand what they're talking about for maybe ten minutes, fork over the check, and forget what they taught me as soon as I get home. I'd rather not have to deal with getting a science tutor.

"No, that's okay. I'll just study harder."

"You can study this weekend."

"Actually, I was wondering if I could go to a party this weekend? Lisa Katz is having the whole class over, and Greg won't stop talking about it."

"I always liked Lisa. Should you take her a gift? I think it's only right you take her a gift."

"It's not that kind of party, Mom."

"Is Greg going to pick you up?"

"I don't know."

Dad decides to chime in. "What boy is picking you up? Why?"

"Greg. You know he's harmless. We're just friends and we're going to a party."

"No boy is harmless, especially around my daughters. We should have sent you to an all girls school."

Ha! I would *really* never get any work done.

"Oh, Dad, you're being silly," Nahal says. "Leila's just a baby. She's not interested in boys."

As far as I know, Nahal's had one serious boyfriend, but she never mentioned him to my father or brought him to the house. Mom knew about him, and I'm pretty sure she was planning their wedding in her head until Nahal came home one day, crushed. I'd never seen her upset like that, especially since she's always ridiculously perfect at anything she does. Things always seem to go her way. Deep down, when that happened, I was pleased to know that she isn't always able to achieve everything she wants.

"The fewer boys around you, the better," Dad says. I want to tell him that won't be a problem.

"Speaking of parties, we've all been invited to the Zamanfars' in two weeks," Mom says, and the three of us groan.

"We have to go!" Mom says laughing. "We're going to Farzaneh's wedding in a few months and the groom's parents want to meet everyone."

"I think I'm on call that weekend," Dad says, winking at me.

"If you are, we'll take separate cars, and if you get paged, you can leave," Mom states. Dad struck out.

"Is Sepideh going to be there?" Nahal asks. Sepideh

is Farzaneh's younger sister, Nahal's age. They have known each other since birth because our parents are close family friends. Nahal and Sepideh *hate* each other. They have this really weird competitive relationship where they try to outdo each other in everything.

"Yes! You two will have so much to catch up on," Mom says. She doesn't seem to understand that Nahal doesn't want to catch up on anything with Sepideh. I just don't want to go because I end up babysitting whatever little kids happen to be around . . . but the food is always good.

"I'm not going to be forced to dance, right?" I ask. After dinner there is always some Persian dance music straight out of Tehrangeles, and several older ladies start dancing and drag in whatever poor suspecting teenagers are around. It's beyond embarrassing. There is no way I am dancing.

"It's rude not to go. We're going and that's that," Mom says. The three of us groan again in defeat.

FIVE

"Sweetie, it's time to get up."

"Uh-huh," I mumble as I open my eyes. Mom leaves and I curl back up again. Waking up for school is painful for me. This is step one of our regular routine.

When she comes back, she's a little more direct. "Honey, you really have to get up, or you'll be late." I know she's right, but I just can't get myself to do it.

"Mmm-hmmm," I say, tugging the comforter over my head.

By the third time the niceness is over. "Leila, you are going to be late! You always do this! You should be more responsible. When I was your age I walked miles to school . . ." etc.

The reward for getting out of bed is the shower. I'm absolved of the previous day's sins, wondering if today might take a different turn, if I can reinvent myself, if I can maybe get myself to be more interested in soccer. Then I towel off and forget about it.

Mom usually has what she wants me to wear laid out on my bed, like I'm four, but I appreciate it. I don't have any fashion sense, and with our dress code it's nice to know I have an endless supply of khakis. Boys have to wear collared shirts, tucked in, slacks, and a tie. Girls can't wear jeans or any skirt above the knee, but some do it all the time. I put on makeup so any zits are hidden, I put product in my hair so it won't kink and frizz out, and I button up my J.Crew shirts, pale yellow or white. It's a costume that lets me blend in as best I can, in spite of my tan skin and black hair.

On Thursdays we have class assembly first thing. Tess's dad, Mr. Carr, runs the show for the junior class along with Ms. Taylor, and they make announcements while everyone ignores them, busily finishing homework or memorizing notes scribbled on index cards for a quiz later on. Today, though, no one is doing anything but looking at the front of the room. Mr. Carr is introducing a new student, and this girl will have our attention for as long as she wants it.

It's clear the class has never seen anything like her

before. *I've* never seen anything like her before. She's wearing a black turtleneck, jeans (which are against dress code), and black heels. She looks like she just walked out of a Garnier Fructis shampoo commercial. She is stunning. Her honey-tinted skin and long dark hair have Robert Peters and others in his group nudging one another, and Ashley Martin sizing her up, taking note of her latest threat.

"Okay, class, we have a new student. Her name is Saskia Lansing and she has just moved here from Switzerland. Saskia, would you care to introduce yourself?"

"Ugh. I hate when Dad does this," Tess whispers in my ear. "It's always so embarrassing, putting someone on the spot." I just wait for Saskia's voice.

"Hello, everyone. I'm very pleased to meet all of you. I've heard a lot of excellent things about your curriculum. Please take pity on me and invite me to lunch for a chat. I'm interesting and charming, I promise."

Saskia smiles and seems so comfortable in her own skin. She looks and acts like she's in her twenties. Poised but not rigid, refined but not stuck up. The announcements keep coming out of Mr. Carr's mouth, and I can feel Tess squirming, unable to deal with whatever her dad is saying.

I can't keep my eyes off Saskia. I'm sure she'll end up dating Robert and start wearing short pink skirts and Ralph

Lauren polo shirts. Maybe she'll even wear one of those ugly acid pink-and-green "we're off to the country club" outfits. Then they'll go to prom together, get married, have babies and—oh my God, she's looking at me. Crap, what do I do? Do I avert my eyes? No, it's too late for that. Okay. Smile, but not too eager, just a subtle—oh my God, she's smiling back. I look around, thinking maybe she's smiling at someone behind me. I turn back to her and she smiles again, this time more widely at my confusion.

Assembly ends and Tess and I wait for everyone to file out. Saskia is talking to Mr. Carr as though they're old colleagues.

"Ah, ladies, this is Saskia. Saskia, this is my daughter, Tess, and her friend Leila Azadi."

"Oh, I love your hair! It's so dark, like mine," Saskia says to me. She smiles as she shakes my hand. "Let me guess, you're Armenian?" I'm a bit taken aback, as no one at school really asks about my heritage.

"Persian, actually." Most people then say, "Oh, like the *Shahs of Sunset*?"

"I love Rumi's poetry! So gorgeous, I wish I could read the original Farsi," Saskia says. She knows about the Persian poet Rumi? It's like finding a magical unicorn in a high school full of cattle.

"Tess is going to show you around this period," Mr. Carr says. I had completely forgotten that Mr. Carr and Tess were standing with us.

"Actually, Dad, maybe Leila can tour Saskia around. I have homework I still need to finish."

"Well, take good care of her, Leila. Let her know what Armstead is all about."

Saskia widens her eyes at me and I try my best not to throw up.

SIX

Act cool. Just act cool and don't let on that you think she is gorgeous. "And over there is the science building but language classes are in there too, which doesn't really make sense since it's a science building but I guess language is a science in itself and you know it takes a certain amount of practice and all."

"You don't have to be so nervous, you know. It is just a campus." Saskia grins as I blush.

"Sorry. I'm not really good at giving tours." Especially giving tours to a really good-looking, Rumi-loving, soon to be "cool" kid.

"Nonsense. You're doing a wonderful job. I now know what teachers to avoid, which boys will try and get into my pants, and what every building is for. But I don't know much about you." Me? She wants to know about me?

"There's not much to tell. After selling off my share in the drug cartel, I've been undercover at this high school. I'm actually thirty-three but nobody knows. Don't tell."

"Your secret is safe with me."

I wish my secret were safe with you. God, stop that! She's probably straight. I wish I had gaydar. I wish it were something you could pick up in a store.

"So what's Switzerland like?"

"Very beautiful, but we were only there for about six months. Dad has to move a lot with his work. He's also in the drug business."

I look at her as though she's kidding, but her face is dead serious.

"Oh . . . wow. Um . . . well . . . people need to get high, I guess." She laughs again.

"He's in pharmaceuticals, silly. He promises this is our last move, but I'm not so sure."

As we talked during our walk around campus, I learned that her dad is Dutch, and her mom is Brazilian, which accounts for her exotic looks and hazelnut skin. She speaks Dutch, Portuguese, Spanish, and some French.

"Do people always ask you where you're from?" Saskia asks me. I know exactly what she means.

"Because I'm ethnically ambiguous? Absolutely," I say, and she giggles. "Mostly, people think I'm Latina and speak to me in Spanish. When I tell them I don't understand, they think I'm denying my heritage or something." This gets her to laugh tremendously. I want to continue to hear it. "Then I say 'No, Middle Eastern,' and the response is always *'Lo siento,'* like I've got it really bad."

"You're adorable," she says as she wipes her eyes. *I am?* "I get asked all the time, too, and now I've lived in so many countries, I never know how to answer people. I just say I'm from outer space and see how they react." I should try that next time. It's nice to be able to talk to someone about this stuff. Tess and Greg don't get it, because people see basic white or black when they look at them. It's the ambiguity that throws people; they want to know which box to put you in.

"I like you," Saskia says offhandedly. "Let's see if we're meant to be friends. Favorite movie?"

"How can a person just pick one?"

"Easy," she says. "Mine's *One Flew Over the Cuckoo's Nest*. Now you have to answer," she says matter of fact.

"There's no way to choose one! I can't even choose which Hitchcock movie I like the best!"

"That's easy, too. It's *Suspicion*," she says.

"You're absolutely wrong about that."

"Don't tell me you're going to go with *Psycho* like other Hitchcock novices," she says while covering her pretend yawn with her hand. I hold my chest in faux shock.

"How dare you! *Strangers on a Train* is far superior." I'm impressed. Greg is only into sci-fi and Tess likes her *Planet Earth* documentaries. Saskia's favorite writer is Anaïs Nïn, she listens to Puccini and Cat Power, and she hopes to start a branch of Amnesty International at Armstead.

The more she talks, the more I feel like the cartoon character Goofy, as in "Gawrsh, she's purrrty!" All that's missing are the tweeting birds flying around my head.

"It must be cool getting to start over again," I say. She doesn't answer for a while after that. I guess it's not so cool. "Do you know what you might want to do for an after-school activity?" I try.

"Mr. Carr told me *Twelfth Night* auditions are this week."

"The last play I was in was in the third-grade musical, and they made me the narrator because I was the best at reading. That and I can't sing."

"There's no singing in *Twelfth Night*," she coos. I could be an actress if she wanted—I mean, if I wanted. It isn't that I am opposed to acting—I act every day like I'm fairly well-adjusted. It's the having-an-audience-watching-you bit that terrifies me.

Saskia links arms with me as we walk, and I imagine this is how Dorothy coaxed the Cowardly Lion into going to Oz. Saskia smells of enchanted fruits that God hasn't created yet. "It would be nice to have a friend audition with me," she says. "And we are friends now, I hope." Hyuck! Say something coherent, Goofy! The bell rings as we enter the main building.

She lets go of me and her arm brushes mine. This is normal, a normal thing to happen between friends. Arms brushing. This shouldn't cause butterflies, which may or may not be indigestion. I'm sure it's just indigestion from staring at her gorgeous face and listening to her amazing life.

"Thank you for showing me around, Leila."

"Thanks for getting me out of study hall." I smile and she moves forward, giving me a kiss on each cheek. I'd gone through this motion before, especially at Persian parties when you have to kiss old, fat Persian men and women who have mentioned how much weight you've gained, but this was a completely different kind of double kiss. I want to stay near her forever but rip myself away out of fear. Oh, don't do this! Your cover will be blown.

"I'll see you soon, I hope," Saskia says before she walks away, and I stay in place as Armstead's best and brightest scurry about to their next classes. I guess I have a crush at school now.

I'm so screwed.

I am in a Saskia haze as I make my way to English class. Ms. Taylor is having us critique one another's creative writing essays before we pass them in on Friday. I'm thinking about how I much prefer our creative writing assignments to analysis of whatever book we're reading as I open the classroom door . . . and find Mr. Harris quickly backing away from Ms. Taylor. His cheeks redden and she awkwardly smooths a strand of hair behind her ear. I guess I'm early.

"Oh God, I'm sorry," I blurt.

I close the door quickly and sag against the wall, pretending that didn't just happen. Mr. Harris walks out of the room and smiles at me.

"Just borrowing some chalk, Leila. I'll see you in class."

He takes long strides down the hall. There is no chalk

in his hand. I walk into the room and Ms. Taylor has her back to me, erasing the chalkboard.

"Hi, Leila! Just wiping these chalkboards down. They get so filthy." I bet they do.

"Sorry I'm early," I say.

"Oh no, it's fine! Early bird gets the worm and all that. Mr. Harris was just asking me about my syllabus format. He's thinking of using it for next term."

I don't say anything. They really need to work on their story. Ms. Taylor breathes in heavily and turns toward me. She walks over to her desk and leans against it.

"Who am I kidding? You're a smart girl, Leila. I suppose you've gathered—"

"I know you and Mr. Harris are dating. It's kind of obvious. No offense or anything."

"No it's . . . it's fine. We're just not ready to be public, because kids talk, and then parents talk . . ."

"Ms. Taylor, it's okay."

"It's just a small community. You know how it is."

"I'm not going to say anything," I say seriously.

"Thank you. I appreciate that very much."

She smiles—that glorious smile—and I tear my eyes away, reaching into my backpack for my English binder. The bell rings and the rest of the class meanders into the room, all heading for their usual seats. Robert Peters has a full Gatorade bottle, and Tess pops out her retainer and wipes it off before inserting it in her mouth again.

"Okay, class, please take out your essays. You know the drill—I pair you off and you critique. Remember, constructive criticism, please! This is a supportive environment and your final essays are due this Friday."

Ms. Taylor has started pairing people off when Lisa Katz walks in, late as usual.

"Lisa, please take a seat next to Leila and work together."

Lisa looks at me with trepidation and I shrug. She sits down at the desk next to mine. I don't think Lisa even brings a notebook or binder to school anymore; it's just one other thing she has to remind herself to do. Since her brother's death, she hasn't really cared about school much. She already has to remember to breathe. I think that's enough for her these days.

"I forgot we had to do this today," she whispers. "I can still read your essay, if you want." Well, with *that* kind of enthusiasm . . . I hand her my essay and I read a history paper I wrote for another class.

"Let's just play pretend," I whisper.

Lisa nods and I begin to proofread my paper on the

Byzantine Empire for the third time while she reads my essay. I wrote an essay set in apartheid-era in South Africa, focusing on a young girl on the day Mandela was freed— and I'm worried I bit off more than I can chew. I glance every so often at Lisa to see how she reacts to the story. I get nothing.

After Lisa finishes reading, she hands back my paper without making eye contact. "You have some grammatical errors and your imagery with the bird is a little cheesy. What's the point of it?" She really doesn't kill with kindness.

"It's symbolic." The birds flying at the end! It's symbolic of freedom!

"It's lazy. But other than that, it was pretty good, Lei." She hasn't called me that in years.

"Thanks." I should leave it at that since we barely speak to each other anymore. It just hurts me to see her so neutral about everything. When we were younger she was always excited to play, no matter what the game or activity was. She was the best Connect Four player; we'd play for hours on end while I described the plot of the original Star Wars trilogy. Now she looks like she doesn't have an ounce of play in her. I want to talk to her about it, but it feels like our friendship was a lifetime ago. "I really liked your paper, too," I say, straight-faced.

"Really? You liked how I talked about the thing? You know, the one where something happens to the thing?"

"Yeah. That. Totally," I say with a sly smile.

She smirks and sticks a piece of gum in her mouth, then offers me one, too. Everyone continues to discuss one another's work. I don't really know what to say to Lisa. She was always quiet as a kid, and I don't know what she's interested in other than soccer and whatever Ashley is into.

"You excited for your party tomorrow?" I ask, taking the piece of gum.

She frowns slightly and pulls her bangs in front of her eyes. "Should be thrilling," she says.

"Can I bring anything?"

"No, it's all taken care of. The DJ, the catering, the bartender serving nonalcoholic drinks only to be spiked later . . . That's nice of you, though."

Ms. Taylor says time is up. The gum in my mouth is getting bitter. It tastes kind of good that way.

SEVEN

I have decided to quit soccer and find myself sitting on a bench about to audition for the play. Tess and I were not improving and were going to be benched the whole season as juniors. I tell myself that would be more embarrassing than trying to act. Maybe they'll let us play something small in the background. I am completely nervous, but not so much because of the audition. I wonder where Saskia is.

My stomach is acting up and I am not sure if it's butterflies or nausea. It's probably both. I pretend I'm reading the monologue I'm going to perform, silently rehearsing, but really I'm going nuts, looking for Saskia in every direction.

Focus, Leila, focus. "Hi!" Saskia calls, swatting the

paper away from my face. I scream and she backs away, laughing.

"I didn't mean to scare you!" she says.

"Sorry, I'm just easily startled."

"I can see that." She smiles and sits down next to me on the bench outside the auditorium. "You nervous?"

Of course I am. You're sitting so close to me. "Yeah." My voice cracks. How embarrassing. She cocks her head back, laughing again at my expense. "I guess I'm a little nervous for the audition. I haven't really done this before."

"Me neither. But it should be fun. Nothing to lose, right?"

She stands up and faces me, reaching for my hand.

"Come on. Let's go in."

I smile and take her offered hand. She doesn't let go as we walk down the ramp into the auditorium. Taryn, one of the tech crew, pops out of the side stage door, carrying a prop trunk. "You're in my way," she grumbles.

I know exactly who I would be expected to hang out with if I came out: the theater tech girls. There are three of them who are for sure gay, and I always compare myself with them and think, *Is this my future? Will I become like them, or even date one of them?*

Taryn, gay tech number one, has not smiled once in public. She has a website where she sells T-shirts that say *I screwed Taryn.* She enjoys flame throwing, photography, and particularly taking photos of her friends smashing furniture with baseball bats. And never shaves her legs. Simone, gay tech number two, wears a bandana every day, knits sweaters, and rows on the crew team. I'm pretty sure Christina, gay tech number three, is not only a lesbian but also a vampire.

They are all vegan, they all listen to feminist folk music by the likes of Erin McKeown, and they all work on tech stuff, building sets and setting up lighting cues in the theater. Even Ashley doesn't bother the tech girls, probably because she's afraid of them. I have to give them credit—they're very much themselves, and that's not always easy. But I look at them and I just don't know if we'd get along. And shouldn't we, as part of the lesbian tribe?

I begin to sidestep and expect Saskia to do the same, but she doesn't.

"Manners like that are unbecoming, don't you think?" Saskia asks loudly.

"Move," Taryn says gruffly. "This shit is heavy." She glances at our linked hands. I pull awkwardly away from

Saskia to make a path for Taryn. She skulks by, and Saskia leads us down the ramp.

"She's a gem," Saskia says. "I didn't know they admitted trolls." She walks into the auditorium as though she's been there dozens of times, while I marvel that Saskia's not intimidated by Taryn and wonder why I am. Tess is already sitting near the middle of the auditorium, but Saskia pulls me toward the few rows in the front. I look back at Tess, who points to the empty seat next to her.

"Should we go sit with my friend Tess?" I ask Saskia as we sit down.

"I want to sit up front so the director notices us. We are stars in the making, and we should present ourselves as such," Saskia says. I can't argue with that, can I?

Mr. Kessler, the drama teacher, comes onstage and opens up his notebook while other students file in. Not too many people have shown up—probably about as many as there are roles in the play. Maybe that means no one will have to face rejection. After a few minutes of silence, Mr. Kessler looks up from his notebook and faces us.

"Okay, so I am sure we are all excited about *Twelfth Night*! It's a play by Shakespeare—you may have heard of him. I'm sure he's going to be a big deal someday." No one laughs. "Anyway, this play is one of my favorites. It's a comedy with gender bending and mistaken identity. Kind of like my time at college."

Crickets.

"Okay, so you all have your monologues. Just do your best. Tomas?" Mr. Kessler nods to Tomas Calvin before sitting down in his seat, facing the stage. There are a few kids at Armstead who are out, and no one has been more out and proud than Tomas.

A secret admirer left a beautiful note in Tomas's locker a week after he came out. Apparently the note said how brave Tomas was and how it inspired the secret admirer to grapple with his own feelings. The note asked Tomas to meet his admirer in the school auditorium after school. No one showed up. When Tomas realized he'd been had and left the auditorium, a few guys wearing ski masks sprayed him with Silly String while calling him a fag.

But after that he was taken in by the hot girls in our class, like Ashley and her followers. He was a fun new accessory, something you just *had* to have, the way celebrities adopt babies like they're handbags. I was happy for him, but I resented the crap out of him, too.

Tomas slowly and methodically walks onto the stage as though he is Laurence Olivier. He pauses for much too long in between lines and then says the next line in a big, booming voice. I think it's supposed to be for dramatic effect. Tess goes next—and she is actually really good! She reads the part of Maria, Olivia's gentlewoman, and has done her homework; Tess delivers the speech with meaning, and I can understand most of what Maria is telling me.

When Saskia takes the stage, everyone pays attention. She's going for the role of Olivia, a wealthy love interest, and everything about her is graceful and sophisticated, but I can't get over how blasé she is. Saskia seems to have this ability to be incredibly indifferent to public scrutiny. It's almost like she forgets she's being watched. She reads her piece, and she is eloquent and charming and regal and totally believable as someone in love. She'll probably get the lead.

"Okay, anybody else?" Mr. Kessler asks as he writes in his notebook. I look around and realize everyone has performed but me. If Tess can do it, so can I. These butterflies sure are aggressive little jerks.

I'm nervous, not so much because of the audition but because Saskia is watching me. I don't want her to think I'm awful or melodramatic or quiet or timid. I want to show her I'm someone to contend with, someone worthy.

I am reading the role of Viola/Cesario, a shipwrecked

young woman who dresses up as a man to work for the Duke. The Duke is in love with the noblewoman Olivia and sends Cesario to go express his love for her. Olivia, though, becomes enamored with Cesario, which complicates things. I know what it's like to have a dual persona, so this role was made for me.

I'm reading the part where Viola in her Cesario disguise realizes Olivia's feelings for her. "She loves me, sure; the cunning of her passion invites me in this churlish messenger," I say performing with what feels to me like conviction and daring. "None of my lord's ring! Why, he sent her none. I am the man: If it be so, as 'tis."

I am killing it! I am captivating the audience's attention, and thinking, *Yes, I am this good. I've got this in the bag. Saskia and I will practice scenes together and I will give her pointers, and she will compliment me and make out with me whenever I want.*

Any chance of that happening is gone as I fart loudly. Onstage. In front of everyone.

Only the ringing laughter that fills the auditorium drowns out the clanging of my heartbeat and the buzzing in my ears. In shock, I finish reading the last few lines out of character. "O time! thou must untangle this, not I; it is too hard a knot for me to untie!" As soon as I finish, I flee from the auditorium. Any chance I may have had with Saskia is now decimated. I don't want to look at her as I run out. I don't want to see if she's laughing along with everybody else.

EIGHT

Dinner at Tess's house on Thursday is more awkward than I had expected. Ms. Taylor didn't know I was going to be there, and I'm still not over walking in on her making out with Mr. Harris. Mr. Carr is talking about the boys' varsity football game this week and how his players are really in shape, considering the preseason workouts he's been putting them through. Mrs. Carr pours herself another glass of wine before offering the bottle to Ms. Taylor, who declines. I am sure she doesn't think drinking in front of her students is very responsible. Neither is sucking face with another teacher at school, but maybe that's just me being petty.

"More for me then," Mrs. Carr says as she puts the bottle by her glass. She gives me a wink. Mrs. Carr drinks an awful lot, but I appreciate her "I say what I mean" approach to life, which may be a side effect of all that drinking.

Ms. Taylor hasn't touched much of her food. She cuts up her meat and looks like she's about to dig in, but she never does.

"I tell you, Greg Crawford is one of the best players on our team this year," Mr. Carr says.

Tess squirms in her seat, this time not out of embarrassment for her dad but because Greg has been mentioned. I don't know why she doesn't go for it. Tragic really. After all, they're both straight; it should be so easy for them—if only Tess believed that Greg and I are just friends.

After more preseason football talk, Mr. Carr turns to me. "So how's our new student? Did you give her the grand tour?"

"Oh, Saskia's great. She's really great." I turn my eyes downward and hear Ms. Taylor finally begin to chew.

"You're too pretty to be a teacher," Mrs. Carr blurts. There's just an ounce or two left in the bottom of the wine bottle now. Ms. Taylor looks up and Tess looks mortified. Mrs. Carr isn't done. "My teachers were always nuns. Between you and that science guy, I'm surprised the students learn anything."

Ms. Taylor chokes on her water a little, and even I am blushing.

"Mom!" Tess says.

Mrs. Carr smiles and turns back to Ms. Taylor. "Oh, it's a compliment. How old are you? You look like a student yourself!"

Mr. Carr clears his throat and starts talking about teaching *Madame Bovary*. Tess looks like she wants to disintegrate into the floor, and I think about how something this awesome never happens in school.

Later, Ms. Taylor offers to drive me home from dinner instead of having my mom pick me up. We listen to some folky-pop hybrid, one of those bands that girls at my school love but I can't stand.

"I failed to tell Mr. Carr that I'm a vegetarian," says Ms. Taylor. "The beef was kind of a surprise. I'm starving. Do you mind if we grab some food?"

We pull into a Dunkin' Donuts, where Ms. Taylor orders a bagel with light cream cheese and a latte, and treats me to a chocolate glazed doughnut and a Coolatta.

"I guess neither of us was really talkative at dinner," she says.

"Well, with the Carrs it can be hard to get a word in."

Ms. Taylor laughs at my candor, and I take a bite of my doughnut. I don't worry how I must look in front of her since she has more to be embarrassed about than I do. We're quiet again. She sips her latte and I watch the television mounted on the wall. Nancy Grace sure looks angry.

"I'm really sorry about today, Leila. Mr. Harris and I were in the wrong, and I don't want this to change our dynamic."

"So are you bribing me with a chocolate doughnut so I don't say anything?"

She laughs nervously.

"I already told you, you don't have to worry, Ms. T. I'm not going to say anything. Can I ask you something, though?"

She nods, sipping her coffee.

"What is it about him that you like? I get that he's dreamy and everything, but other than that."

"I don't think we should talk about this. It's not appropriate."

Is she kidding? I take another bite of my doughnut.

She speaks again. "But since you proved your ability to use discretion at dinner . . . I like him because I feel safe around him. He's stable, he wants to have kids one day, and I know he'd be a good dad. All clear?"

It's strange seeing her so honest.

I nod. "You're a great teacher, and if you leave, I'll be stuck with Mr. Carr talking about sports instead of literature. Really, it's in my best interest not to say anything."

She laughs at this. "It's nice being able to talk about it. I mean, we shouldn't be, but it's hard keeping a secret like that."

I shove the doughnut in my mouth, chewing on *my* secret, the one I want to blurt out to someone. Anyone.

"So how are you liking junior year so far?" Ms. Taylor asks. "You seem to be handling the material well, but I'm surprised you don't participate in class more. Your last essay would have made for a great discussion topic—"

"I like girls," I say, sputtering doughnut crumbs. I can't believe I just said it out loud for the first time. It feels ridiculous, frightening, and exhilarating all at once.

"I'm sorry?"

"Shit. This is so awkward," I mumble. "I don't know why I told you."

I can see she is processing what I said. I feel like crawling underneath the table, crouching down there until the manager closes up shop.

"It's okay. I guess we're both speaking in the spirit of honesty today." I want to throw up my doughnut, but Ms.

Taylor holds my hand and I feel a little better. "Do you want to talk about it?"

I shake my head. I'm not ready yet. We leave the Dunkin' Donuts and walk to her car. Whatever teacher-student relationship we had yesterday is gone now. We know too much about each other to go back. We've been driving ten minutes before I find my voice again.

"Do you think we can change the music? I'm not really into these whiny guys."

NINE

"Leila *joon*, Greg is downstairs waiting! Are you ready?"

Mom smooths my hair out when I turn in my chair to face her. She's blow-dried it straight and has fit me into a navy-blue dress for the semiformal party. My C cups runneth over, but I'm sure Greg won't mind.

"Look at how pretty you are!" Mom exclaims. "You should straighten your hair all the time!"

Well, I guess that's one thing I can straighten about myself.

"I better get going."

I walk downstairs and Greg's eyes widen for a moment. Mom, always the good Persian guest, bought me a gift to give to Lisa, even though I told her it's not a birthday party.

Greg opens the passenger side door for me, and I wish this wasn't so obviously looking like a date, especially when Mom waves to us from the house. I just know she's picturing waving good-bye to us on our wedding night.

Greg tunes the radio to Classic Rewind, and the sounds of Journey escort us over to Lisa's house. It's ironic that "Don't Stop Believin'" is on, because from the way Greg occasionally glances at my cleavage, there may be some hope left in him.

"Eyes on the road," I say as I fold my arms over my chest. Greg coughs and I change the radio station in hopes of changing his train of thought. "I had dinner at Tess's last night," I say. "Her dad kept gushing about you." Tess would have, too, but Greg doesn't need to know that.

"Yeah, the team is really holding its own this year."

"Greg, can you at least try and boast a little? If I was a star football player, you wouldn't be able to shut me up."

He laughs quietly. "Trust me. I've seen you on the soccer field. I don't know that the football team would take you." I swat his arm and he laughs louder. "Though you can take a hit. At least from soccer balls, anyway." I fake laugh and then scowl at him, and that makes him laugh even harder.

Lisa's house is pulsing with music. I drop my mother's gift for Lisa on a table in the foyer and look for familiar faces in the crowd. Robert and his guy pals are chugging beer, spilling it all over the Persian rugs. Those things have history, Goddamn it! Ashley is grinding with some hockey guy, while her gal pals look bored to death. It's strange being here again. I feel like Lisa's brother, Steve, should come jogging down the stairs, laughing at all of us and then driving off to the movies with his college girlfriend. I begin to make my way over to Tess.

Greg goes straight for the kill. "Do you want to dance?"

No, I think.

"Sure," I say.

I change course and we head for the dance area. I'm pretty sure Ashley could get arrested for what she's now doing with the hockey player. Greg and I just stare at each other for a moment, and then he begins to move his arms side to side—not at all with the beat of the song. His legs remain immobile except for some strange bending at the knees. This continues for a minute more until I take pity on him and swing my arms over his shoulders to restrain them from any further movement. We sway at a sort of frantic rhythm that still doesn't match the song. Greg's hands are clammy, gripping at my lower back. I wish I were dancing with Saskia. Around her I feel longing, passion, confusion. Greg's hand is now on the top part of my butt. This just feels wrong.

"Greg, I have to go to the bathroom."

"Do you want me to go with you?"

To the bathroom? "No, I'll be fine. Thanks," I say.

I leave him in the dance area and take the back stairs up to the second floor, a space I haven't been in for years. When Lisa and I were younger, we'd go upstairs and talk about school and which teachers we didn't like, about her emotionally unavailable parents and my sister's annoyingly perfect accomplishments. Now, I gently open the door to a balcony, hoping not to find anyone making out. Instead I find Lisa in her sweats, sitting on the balcony, her knees pulled into her chest. She looks up, startled to be found, but she seems relieved that it's only me.

"You do know there's a party in your house, right?"

She nods. "I'd rather not watch my house get trashed."

Her hair is up in a messy ponytail, and even in this disheveled state she looks like a teen magazine queen. I sit down next to her and wrap my arms around myself.

There's a book on the patio next to her. "What are you reading?"

"*A Tree Grows in Brooklyn*. It's kind of slow."

"Yeah, I read that last summer. It's good. You just have to wait it out a little."

We sit in silence for a few moments more, and then I sneeze.

"Jesus, you sound like a dying animal."

I hold up my hands, now covered in snot, and Lisa rolls her eyes and goes inside. Apparently I've repulsed her beyond tolerating my presence. Well, screw her. She's the weirdo ditching her own party.

"Here," she says, suddenly back again, plopping a box of tissues in my lap before sitting back down. I wipe my hands and nose, and then blow loudly.

"Sorry. Nice party."

"Is it? That's good," she says, pulling her bangs in front of her eyes. She sighs and examines her perfectly manicured nails.

"If I knew we could wear sweats to this party, I totally would have worn mine." This doesn't get Lisa to react at all. "You haven't complimented me on my dress," I say.

She doesn't even look at me. "Tell your mom she did a good job picking it out."

"Aw! You remember my lack of fashion sense."

She smirks and finally turns to face me. "Hard to forget. You remember scruff days?"

Scruff days were a fun way for the administration at our elementary school to remind us that we had freedom to dress how we wanted . . . for one day each semester.

"You always looked like a homeless person on crack," she says. "I remember one outfit where your shirt didn't match your pants and you had like four hats on."

"I was cool! I had flavor."

"You had something."

Lisa falls quiet again, staring vacantly out into space.

"Your essay was great the other day," I try. "The one where the thing happened to the thing? You must have spent a lot of time on it."

She continues to stare into space. "Leila, why are you up here?"

"I'm avoiding Greg Crawford. He's working hard to turn our nondate into a date. Why are *you* up here, Lisa?"

She looks at me with a weak smile. "I haven't really felt like socializing much. You know, what with my brother dying and everything." There's a sting in her words, but I know it isn't necessarily directed at me. More at the universe.

"I know I'm being a huge baby and people die all the time, but I feel lonely without him. I feel lonely all the time. And it's been a year, I should be over it, but I'm not."

I don't know what to say. There are no tears, no anger, just complete weariness in her voice. I kind of can't believe she's picked me to open up to.

"And please don't be like everyone else and say you understand or it'll all be okay, because it's not going to bring him back," she says.

"I farted onstage during play auditions today," I say. Diversion. It's all I have to work with right now.

Lisa smiles and shakes her head, so I run with it.

"I didn't plan on it happening, of course. I mean, I was totally in the groove, everyone stunned by my acting ability, and it just sputtered out of me."

"I didn't know you were into theater."

"I'm not. I just thought anything would be better than soccer." I say it like I believe it.

"I hope you're a better actress than soccer player."

She's still wearing her smile, and it's nice to see her be a little lighter.

"Your friends downstairs are grinding up a storm," I tell her, and then make a fake puking noise. "Why do you hang out with them anyway?"

"I don't have to think too much when they're around. We shop or go to parties, but there's no heavy stuff."

That makes sense. We sit there in silence again.

"Do you want to be alone?" I ask.

She doesn't say anything for what feels like a whole minute. "Yeah, if you don't mind."

I stand up to leave when she drops a bombshell. "I can see why you don't like Greg. I don't think he's your type."

Has she figured me out? "What's my type then?" I ask, like I'm vaguely curious to know.

She shrugs and picks up her book. "No clue. But hopefully someone who can help you pick out your outfits." She can't possibly know what that sounds like to me, can she?

I leave the balcony only to be greeted by Mrs. Katz, and I turn red, as though she can tell what I'm thinking.

"Leila. What are you doing up here?"

"Sorry, I was just using the restroom in there. The downstairs one was occupied."

"Oh. Have you seen Lisa?"

"No. Sorry."

Mrs. Katz doesn't even try to make chitchat; she just walks off in the wrong direction to look for her daughter.

Back downstairs I see Ashley giving Greg a lap dance of sorts, and everyone at the party is surrounding them, laughing and clapping. Greg is looking side to side, as if trying to escape. Sparing him any further embarrassment,

I walk over and yank him by his hand. Ashley loses her balance and stumbles to the floor, red-faced and scowling.

"Bitch!" Clever.

"Sorry, he's my ride. I'd better get home," I say with mock friendliness.

"Why? Are you missing something on the SyFy channel?"

I don't reply but just walk away, pulling Greg behind me.

We don't speak on the ride home. I think both of us are embarrassed, for different reasons.

"I was having a good time you know," Greg huffs as he turns left.

"You looked uncomfortable dancing with her. I thought I was helping," I say. I didn't even want to go to the party!

"Well, at least she was interested in me," Greg mutters. I thought we were over this! Does he think I'll change my mind about liking him?

"Greg, you *should* be with someone who is interested in you." It's just not me. We get to the house and Greg leans across me to open the door. "I'll see you Monday," he says. He's not going to walk me to the house, I can see.

I give him an unenthusiastic salute and walk to the door, remembering why I've never been a fan of parties.

TEN

Sunday at lunch, Dad continues to compliment Nahal on her day at the hospital, especially how attentive she was during the surgery when she observed him in the operating room. I keep pushing all the saffron-coated rice around the chicken and dried barberries to one side of my plate, saving the best for last.

"Nahal was so observant!" Dad exclaims. "All the nurses and residents were so impressed!"

Mom is smiling giddily, no doubt envisioning her daughter in scrubs, rushing around performing complicated, miraculous surgeries and still being home at night to see the perfect kids she'll have with her perfect husband. They'll all play board games together on weekends, set up low-key barbecues, maybe have golden retrievers named Rusty and Scout. Whenever I go over to visit my sister and her dashingly handsome and successful husband, they'll ask me what I'm up to, and I'll tell them I'm feeling pretty good since I moved into a bigger box off the side of the highway. Much better digs than that dump in the Store 24 parking lot. They'll offer me something to eat and I will hoard things, stuffing bread and raw hot dogs in my pockets for later, frightening my nephews and nieces.

The dogs will growl and try to scare me off, but they won't know the things I've seen, won't know what scrapes I've gotten into. That's when I'll realize I'm allergic to dogs. My eyes will water, turn fiery red, and my face will break out in hives, blinding me in a puffy, dirty, homeless, lesbionic state. Cowering in the grass of their beautiful backyard, my mother will cry out: *"Oh, if only she were good at science like you, Nahal! If only she dated Greg back in high school! My poor, poor Leila!"*

"Leila," Nahal says.

I twitch as if I've been hit by lightning. "I don't want to be homeless!" I shout.

"Jeez. Leila, what's your problem?" Nahal and our parents stare at me.

"Nothing. Sorry." I slump in my chair.

"What are you talking about, Leila *joon*?" Dad begins to laugh and everyone else joins in, my spontaneous out-burst diverting some attention from Nahal at least, though not for the right reasons.

"I guess I was just rehearsing for the play. If I get a part," I say.

"What play? What about soccer?" Mom is clearly con-cerned that I will no longer be forced to work out, and will gain weight.

"I quit soccer and auditioned for the school play in-stead. I'll find out this week if I made it."

"So you might not even have a part?" says Nahal.

Why are you even here, Nahal? I think. *Don't you have any friends?*

"No. I just said I don't know yet," I say. "I'll find out this week."

"What will you do if you don't get a part?" Mom chimes in, hoping there will be some other masochistic physical activity after school.

"I guess I'll help behind the scenes or something. I thought it might be fun to do something different. Why is everyone giving me a hard time?"

"Leila, calm down. We just want to know what's going on in your life," says Nahal like she's my mother. *Nahal, shut up, and stop condescending to me just because you don't have a social life.*

"The play is *Twelfth Night*," I say. "It's Shakespeare. So really, it's educational—and you're always saying how education is the most important thing," Hopefully this will shut everybody up.

"If it's something you like, Leila *joon*, then we will support you no matter what. We will sit in the front row every night with flowers." Mom smiles and puts more salad on my plate.

"*If* she gets a part," my premenstrual sister says. I can't believe Nahal and I are even related. I'm surprised Dad hasn't commented on the situation. He usually chimes in about how important school is and how he hopes other activities won't get in the way of my already mediocre science grades. But he just frowns and chows down more saffron chicken and barberries. Dad and I don't have much in common, but our few similarities are strong. You can read exactly how we're feeling from our facial expressions and we can't hide our emotions at all. Nahal, of course, is the first to mention it.

"Daddy, what's wrong?" Why does she even call him "Daddy" anymore? She's not four.

"I just don't see why Leila would seriously consider theater. Is this a career path for you?" Dad asks.

"Uh . . . I don't know, Dad. It's just a school play," I say.

"I mean, do you want to be an actor? That's not a real job," he says with a chuckle.

"I wasn't planning on becoming a professional soccer player but no one complained about that. And if I were considering acting as a job, so what? What's wrong with that?" I could be a great character actor. Bag lady with crazy hair, Latina maid, terrorist, I could do it all.

"Only drug addicts and gays are actors. You don't want to hang out with those people, do you?" the good doctor asks.

That knocks the wind out of me. I understand it's a cultural thing, and my father is a traditional, conservative Iranian man, but I've never heard him explicitly say something like that. I don't want to hang out with those people. Imagine if he knew I *am* one of those people.

"Daddy, not all actors are gays or drug addicts! What about Clint Eastwood? You love his movies," Nahal says.

"That was a different time, and you want to see your sister in a cowboy outfit shooting people? Medicine is a consistent profession. No matter what the economy is like, there is always work. How else do you think I could afford to keep all you women in such comfort?"

"You're right, Daddy," Nahal says with a smile, and sips from her glass of water.

"I have homework to do. May I be excused?" I ask Mom, who nods. I walk upstairs and lie on my bed, playing a few mind-numbing rounds of Tetris on my laptop, trying to make the pieces fit. I'm always trying to make the pieces fit.

Mom comes up later with a plate of cut-up watermelon and pears. I don't pretend that I'm working. I'm just in front of the computer, looking at past high scores.

"Eat this fruit. It's good for your skin." She puts the plate on the table and sits next to me on the bed. "I'm sure you will get a part. I think it's good for you to try new things. It shows character, and maybe you'll really learn more about yourself."

"Yeah, maybe."

Mom takes a slice of pear from the plate and hands it over to me. I chew on it slowly, and I wish this heavy feeling in my stomach would go away.

"Your father works hard for a living," Mom says. "He just wants to make sure you have a good life and can support yourself." I smile a little and take another bite of pear. "I wish you would talk to me more, Leila. These days I feel like you don't share as much with me as you used to."

I'm afraid you and Dad are going to hate me.

I'm afraid everyone will hate me.

"If something's bothering me, I'll let you know, Mom," I say.

"I hope so." She smiles sadly before walking away, and I start a new game.

ELEVEN

I'm an understudy in the play. Fair enough. I didn't even finish my audition. But I have to learn all of the main characters' lines *and* act as stage manager because I need something to do while the regular cast is rehearsing. Not only does Tess have the lead role of Viola/Cesario, but Saskia is playing Olivia, the character who moons over Cesario. In other words, Saskia has to act like she's in love with Tess Carr in drag, while I wait in the wings. How could this happen? I should be comforted that I am not the only one who wasn't cast in the play. Tomas Calvin, who poured his heart into his audition, is also an understudy/stage manager. Of course that means we have to work together. Great.

Tomas devotes most of our first rehearsal to complaints. "I can't believe I didn't get a part. I mean *you* I can understand, because, well, that was just embarrassing. But me, I have so much talent!" I half listen to him as I look over the binder full of notes and stage-blocking diagrams. I can't believe I signed on for this.

"I would be a perfect Sebastian," Tomas continues. "It doesn't make sense that they cast Nick Fullerton instead of me! He breathes through his mouth and always scratches his balls like no one will notice. Not that I've noticed. Well, okay, maybe I have, but he brings that attention on himself."

Having to work with Tomas must be some sort of punishment for my recent negative energy. Now I have all the proof I need that my entire life is a sitcom designed by God for His personal enjoyment. Tomas and I sit in the midsection of the empty auditorium, watching Mr. Kessler get the actors organized in a circle for some stupid bonding activity. Saskia walks in at the last minute and glides over to the stage as though she isn't late at all, smiling at everyone. As Mr. Kessler leads the group in activity, Tomas continues to whisper to me.

"I heard the new girl's parents are loaded."

"So what if they are?" I whisper back. "It's none of our business."

It's the first sentence I've said in about half an hour of Tomas's whining, and of course it's in defense of Saskia.

Tomas is ready to move on anyway. "I was thinking there's going to have to be one stage manager behind stage with props and things, and one in the tech booth. And since I am clearly more of a conversationalist, I think it's only appropriate that I work with the actors and you work with the techies."

"No," I say emphatically.

"Why not? Chicken?"

"Yes. I am. You guessed it."

"Leila, don't be unreasonable. I mean, you know gay men and hard-core lesbians like the tech girls don't get along."

Tomas and I glance behind us where the tech girls are looking over plans for constructing the sets. Simone is knitting absurdly long stockings while Taryn goes over diagrams and Christina bares her fake set of vampire fangs. Christina glances in our direction and bites harshly into her apple. Tomas and I turn back around quickly and in sync.

"They'll kill me, Leila! You're a woman. They'll take pity on you! Maybe even hit on you!"

"Shut up, Tomas."

Saskia is making the other actors laugh. I wish I could hear what she's saying.

"I so want to be friends with her!" Tomas is giddy to a stereotypical T.

"What happened to Ashley and all of them?"

"They're boring. This new girl is so . . . exotic and traveled. Plus she dresses so cosmopolitan chic." Saskia does a dramatic twirl for her part in the bonding exercise and everyone else in the group has to do the same motion. "What do you think of her?" asks Tomas.

What a loaded question. I think she's gorgeous, enigmatic, and unlike anyone I will ever meet, unlike anyone I will inquire or dream about, unlike anyone worth mentioning in magazines and literature.

"She's nice," I murmur.

"Well, I'm going to be friends with her." As irritating as I find Tomas, there is one thing that I really admire about him. He is sincerely sure about everything.

After rehearsal Tomas and I are left to clean up the stage and put the props back in their places, that sort of thing. The role we share is about as important as a calculator during a history exam. Though I will admit this: It's better than soccer.

Tomas has wandered off and I'm onstage sweeping up when Saskia walks toward me. My breath quickens.

"Hi! You look like a Middle Eastern Cinderella!"

"Hi, Saskia."

"I'm sorry we won't get to act together."

"It's okay. I think I'm doing a good job at this sweeping thing, don't you?" I smirk and she grins back. I could play this game for years.

"It's too bad really. You did have a tremendous audition."

"Please, I'm embarrassed enough as it is. There's no reason for you to rub salt in the wound."

"Oh please, everybody farts. The stuff before that was absolutely brilliant."

"You think so?"

"Of course! I don't say something unless I mean it." That's a philosophy I could stand to live by. "What are you doing this weekend?" she asks out of the blue.

"I have a family thing I have to do." I really don't want to go to the Zamanfars'. But I suppose if I don't, I'll be home watching a Lifetime movie marathon and fantasizing about my first date with Saskia.

"Are you free next weekend?" she asks casually. "I was wondering if you'd like to come by my place. My parents are hardly ever in town and I could use some company."

My stomach takes the express elevator from the basement to the penthouse.

"I'd love to."

"So would I!" Tomas says as he comes bounding toward us.

"Tomas gave me the idea for all of us to hang out!" Saskia exclaims. "I'm so looking forward to it."

I don't believe it—he's actually achieving his goal!

"Well, I better go. See you!" Saskia waves and runs down the ramp, out of the auditorium.

"We are going to have so much fun, Leila!" says Tomas. "I'm going to bring my cocktail book and everything." He drops a boxful of props by my feet and smiles. "Would you mind putting these away tonight? I'm just going to go chat with Saskia before she leaves. Bye!"

"I know. I can't stand that guy, either," Taryn says from behind me. I swear she just appeared. She pops out of places like a phantom. She picks up the box of props and puts it in the cabinet backstage while I pretend to sweep some more. "You like her, don't you?"

"What?"

"New girl. You have a crush on her."

"I . . . I'm not like that."

Taryn's cold look doesn't change during all this, but she nods in understanding.

"Guess I'm just seeing things. My bad."

She skulks away and leaves me alone in the auditorium.

TWELVE

I keep fidgeting with my dress and wish I could just wear pants to this thing. Mom insisted I should wear a purple bebe she found on sale. She doesn't play around when it's Persian Party Time, and a Persian designer is a nice plus.

Dad drives and Mom sits up front while Nahal and I sit in the back. "Zohreh says Farzaneh met her fiancé in dental school." Mom is gushing as she relays what her friend Zohreh has told her about her future son-in law. "He comes from a good family in Los Angeles. His father is a professor at UC Riverside, and his mother is an electrical engineer."

"You know why people become dentists? They can't get high enough marks to become real doctors—right,

Nahal?" Dad says it with fresh conviction, like we haven't been hearing this joke for years.

"Don't say that at the party!" Mom commands, and Dad just nods. "Anyway, he's supposed to be handsome."

"I bet he's gross like her last boyfriend." Nahal's not wrong, that guy was gross.

"Nahal, that's not nice," Mom reprimands her. The last boyfriend always left his top shirt buttons undone to show his flowing chest hair. He also fancied himself an "entrepreneur," though no one actually knew what he did for a living. Farzaneh has always dated Persian guys. Whether it's because she's truly attracted to them or because her parents expect her to marry a Persian man, I haven't a clue. Mom and Dad have never imposed upon Nahal and me that we should have only Persian significant others. But I'm sure they assume someone of the opposite sex, at least, is a given.

"What's Farzaneh's fiancé's name?" I ask.

"Oh, um . . . It's uh . . . hmmm, I forget!" Mom says. She knows all his accolades have been rattled off but doesn't know his name, which is less important. I'm sure he has two names, the Persian name that his parents bestowed upon him and his day-to-day American name. A lot of Iranians have names that are difficult for some people to pronounce, like Khosro, so they'll go by something like "Kevin" at their jobs or among friends. The best is when the Persian name has nothing to do with the Western name. When Parviz becomes Mark, I'm not really sure where that comes from.

We drive up to the massive McMansion that is the Zamanfars' home, and Dad parks the car. "Everybody ready?" Mom asks with a wide smile.

When we enter everyone stands up and we greet each other individually. There is a lot of kissing on both cheeks; you can't overlook anyone. So anytime someone enters a party, there's more standing and kissing.

"*Salam, Leila joon! Che bozorg shodi!* You're growing up so fast," says a lady whose name I don't remember, though I know she has a son my age, which she mentions to my mom *all* the time. I might as well wear a beauty pageant sash that says *Prospective Bride*. I would *die*.

Mom has me sit next to her while she speaks to some ladies whose names I kind of remember but not really. They're all speaking in Farsi about the usual—their families, the health of their family members, any future marriages in the community, births of acquaintances' adult children, etc.

I end up nodding and smiling a lot. I'm embarrassed by how rudimentary my Farsi is and how long it takes me to come up with certain words. Not to mention my horrendous American accent, which leaves me unable to pronounce guttural *g* sounds. At least I understand everything people say, so I can be on alert if they are saying anything about me.

"*Kodoum daneshgah mikhai bereed?*" asks a friendly old lady. Which college do I want to go to? I haven't thought about college yet, though I am sure everyone expects me to be as ambitious as Nahal. I'm ambitious enough to put hair gel in my curls each morning and that's about it.

"*Insha' Allah een tabestoon fehkreh daneshgah miko-nam,*" I say. *God willing, this summer I will think about colleges* is what I think I said. Definitely not Nahal's alma mater, but the way Dad talks to his friends you'd think I was a genius.

The men usually all sit together and talk about work, the news, and—mostly—stories of the old days in Iran or people they knew from back then. Most of them didn't even grow up in the same parts of Iran or know one another there. Dad is from Tehran, but his best friend here in the United States, Dr. Kotoyan, is Armenian Iranian, and they met at the hospital where they work. The doctors humor and are willing to speak with the lawyers, accountants, small business owners, and finance barons. Some drink alcohol, others don't. Some are Muslim, some are Christian, some are Jewish, and a few families are Baha'i. They all have just one thing in common, the country they are from.

The men are engrossed in conversation, and Dad is playing a rousing game of backgammon with Dr. Kotoyan, cheering and laughing at every roll of the dice. It's nice getting to see him let loose a little. He works long hours, not that I mind—it's been like that since always. When he gets called to the emergency room late at night or has to work really long hours, I always think of him as Bruce Wayne looking out into the night sky and seeing the Bat-Signal. Only if Bruce Wayne were five nine, older, had a darker complexion, and was always cracking jokes about dentists.

I try to stay engaged in the conversation with the women. Nahal speaks in her almost perfect Farsi to Zohreh, Farzaneh's and Sepideh's mom. I can't hear what they're saying, but Nahal is making Zohreh laugh. Every time we come to one of these things, Nahal is just so good at saying all the right things and being the proper young woman. She never slouches, is well dressed, and is studying just the right thing at the best university in the world. All the women at these events eat that stuff up like it was *tadig*, the crispy rice dripping with oil that tastes so good.

Nahal always obliged when Mom and Dad signed her up for Saturday-morning Farsi classes, and I always hated going because they interrupted Saturday-morning cartoons. I eventually quit, but Nahal went all through elementary school, middle school, and high school. I could never tell if she did it because she enjoyed it or because it delighted Mom and Dad.

"Leila, why don't you go see what the other kids are up to?" Mom asks, sensing my boredom. By *kids* she means the children of the older people here; we range in age from thirty-four to sixteen. Then there are the *little kids*, whose parents are second-generation Iranian American. Zohreh shows Nahal and me into the den, where some of the *kids* have found sanctuary from the plethora of questions.

"Hey, guys," I say to familiar faces I see every couple of months when we make the rounds to all the parties.

"Hi, ladies!" Sepideh says, oozing faux cheeriness. She air-kisses me on both cheeks and then flits over to Nahal to do the same.

"Hi, Sepideh! It's so nice to see you again," Nahal says so warmly that you would never know that the two are sworn enemies who have hated each other since childhood. Zohreh tells us all to have a great time and leaves the motley crew to hang out.

"Did you meet Farzaneh's fiancé yet?" Sepideh asks Nahal as they sit down next to each other on a leather couch. "He's so wonderful."

"No! Not yet, but I've heard so many wonderful things.

Are you excited for the wedding?" I don't know why they do this. Pretend to like each other. As soon as we get in the car to go home Nahal is just going to complain about how fake Sepideh is and all the things she can't stand about her.

"So excited!" Sepideh coos. "I have the most *beautiful* dress. I was telling Shahram that I can't wait for *our* wedding. Once he's finished business school and I've finished law school. Did I tell you I'm going to law school at Brown?" I can see Nahal wince only slightly, but that's because I know her facial expressions so well. It kills Nahal that Sepideh has a Persian boyfriend, not because Nahal wants one, but because it will trump almost everything Nahal does. Well, all except for . . .

"Congratulations! I still have a year of pre-med, but hopefully I'll figure out where I'll go for medical school soon. I'd like to continue studying medicine at Harvard, but you know, med school competition being so stiff and everything . . . ," Nahal says, a genuine smile on her face. Medical school will always trump law school. Period.

Sepideh's smile doesn't waver. "Oh, I'm sure you'll be just fine, Nahal. But with all that studying, will you ever find time to meet guys?" This is getting really uncomfortable. I leave them to it and walk over to Parsa, a college freshman, and his brother, Arsalan, who's my age. They're arguing about whether LeBron James is the greatest basketball player to ever play the game.

"If LeBron played one-on-one with Kobe, LeBron would win. One hundred percent," Arsalan says with finality.

"That's the dumbest thing I've ever heard. You know how many championship rings Kobe Bryant has? Five! You know who has one more than Kobe? Do you?" Parsa goads his brother, because he knows that Arsalan knows the answer.

"Michael Jordan," Arsalan mutters under his breath.

"What's that? I didn't hear you?" Parsa yells. This is my Saturday night. I could be hanging out with Saskia. *Saskia!* We'd be having lots of intelligent conversation about film and music, maybe accidentally brush arms again . . .

I mosey over to the little kids watching a Pixar movie. Roksana, who goes by Roxy, is ten and the ringleader of eight-year-old twin girls and a five-year-old boy who at the moment are entranced by racing cars rounding a track.

"Hi, Roxy," I venture.

"Hi," she says, but her eyes never leave the screen. I watch the movie silently with them until dinner is announced.

The dinner spread on the dining table is massive as usual. Giant platters heaped with basmati rice with saffron, more rice with raisins and lentils, and *lubia polo*—rice with ground beef and green beans in a sauce made of turmeric, cumin, cinnamon, onion, and tomato paste. Then there are skewers and skewers of *koobideh kabob*, *kabob barg*, and chicken *kabob* as well as and three different stews.

"Do you think this will be enough food for everyone?" Zohreh asks my mother as they bring out the *mast-o-khiar* and the *kashk-e-bademjan* from the kitchen. Is she kidding? There's enough food for Fenway Park. Hospitality is never in short supply in Persian homes. Among Persians, the more a person loves you, the more they want to shove food down your throat.

I *tarof* with an older gentleman in front of me waiting to fill his plate with grub.

"After you," I insist to the man.

"No! I wouldn't dream of it," the man says, and this goes on for about two minutes. *Tarof* is when you offer something out of respect, even if you don't really mean it. Like when my mom goes to lunch with Zohreh and they both insist on paying the bill. It takes about twenty minutes before one of them steals the bill and runs to the server with a credit card. I didn't get that *tarof* was a Persian thing as a little kid—so when I offered other kids my toys to play with, I thought they'd decline the offer and offer their toys as well. That never happened, and I always ended up playing with some toy I didn't really want to or giving away toys I loved.

The older man finally concedes and goes ahead of me, and we all mill about the table, loading the goodies onto our plates. I reach for a set of silverware and my hand brushes with an older woman's hand.

"Oh, *bebakshid*," I say, excusing myself and looking up to see Mrs. Madani, who appears much older than the last time I saw her, three years ago.

"*Salam, Leila joon,*" she says, and hands me a fork and knife rolled up in a paper napkin. Her wrinkles are deeper, especially around her mouth, and even though she is wearing a lot of eye makeup, she doesn't have on enough foundation to hide her dark circles.

"How are you?" I almost ask her how her son Kayvon is doing, but I am quick to catch myself. She studies my face for a moment and smiles sadly.

"Okay, thank you," she says. The "thank" sounds like "*tank*" because of her heavy accent. She used to brag about her son all the time; you couldn't get her to shut up about him. Same for Mr. Madani. Now he sits near the other men, his hair thinning, his eyes sunken, and his posture rigid, like he's ready to fight if provoked.

Mr. Madani used to talk about how good a tennis player Kayvon was, how he was an excellent student. "My son is going to be the next Agassi," he would say, and Kayvon would shake his head in embarrassment and ask me if I wanted to play video games. I liked Kayvon well enough. He always seemed interested in things I had to say and didn't treat me like a little kid. It was nice watching Nahal and Sepideh have their brag-offs, and then going off together to mimic them in private.

"Did I tell you? I'm going to the moon for NASA next week!" Kayvon would say in a falsetto voice.

"The moon is so yesterday. I'm going to be orbiting Jupiter next month," I would reply, flipping my hair the way Nahal does. Kayvon is Nahal's age. Three years ago he started going to Tufts, still living at home. Then suddenly we didn't hear about him anymore.

We found out through the Persian rumor mill that someone saw Kayvon kissing another guy at a college party. I don't know who started the rumor or if there was a photo online or something, but he had to come out to his parents. They didn't take it well.

I overheard Mom talking on the phone a couple of years ago about how she couldn't believe the Madanis kicked Kayvon out of the house. That gave me a bit of hope, but she never said a word to Nahal or me. For a while I kept hoping someone would mention it—maybe talk about how much they liked Kayvon, or how much they missed him, but the Madanis still come to all the parties, and it's like Kayvon never existed. No one mentions him, because they don't want to upset the Madanis.

As we all eat, Farzaneh, the bride, sits next to her fiancé on a couch, answering questions from the throngs of older women about their wedding and marriage.

"When are you two going to start having babies?" an old lady asks Farzaneh.

"Hopefully, you'll have boys. Boys are princes," old lady number two says, eyeing Farzaneh's general uterus area like she is willing a boy to show up in there.

After I finish the food piled on my plate, I walk back into the den and plop myself next to Roxy in front of the TV. She absently shoves rice in her mouth, spilling a few grains on the rug beneath her.

"Are they still humble-bragging?" I whisper, and Roxy turns her head to observe Sepideh and Nahal not touching their food and speaking with their hands about God knows what. I know it is killing Nahal, because she loves *lubia polo*, and the only thing keeping her from devouring it is she that she's waiting for Sepideh to take a bite first.

Roxy turns her attention back to the television. "Yeah. When the movie's over, you want to play hide-and-seek?" The other little kids look at me eagerly, and I know how I'll spend the rest of the evening.

THIRTEEN

Monday morning in study hall I can't focus because Tess keeps asking about Lisa's party. "Do you think Ashley likes Greg?" she says as she continues to not so subtly inquire about her crush while we sit at our worktable in the library. She stares off at Greg, who is studying nearby. It's a gaze out of a Jane Austen novel, full of yearning and patience. Yuck.

"I don't know, Tess. Maybe *you* should ask him out already," I say.

"What? I was just curious." Tess is a great actress onstage, but her acting here is as convincing as an infomercial.

"Tess, you so obviously do. Just go for it!"

"Is it that obvious?"

"Probably not to anyone but me. You really have nothing to lose."

She doesn't say anything. I sigh like Charlie Brown. "There is honestly *nothing* going on between me and Greg. You have my blessing to suck his face." Tess blushes profusely and I chuckle.

"What if he doesn't like me?"

"What are you really scared of? You're a catch!"

"I don't know. It's just that I know he was so into you, and I don't feel like being a consolation prize."

I get that sometimes Greg thinks he still likes me, but only because he hangs out with me and doesn't know about all the girls who like *him*. Maybe if he saw who else was out there for him, I'd never have to worry about feeling like I'm leading him on. I get up, facing Greg. Tess grabs my arm. "Where are you going?"

"Relax, jeez, I'm just going to the bathroom."

Her grip loosens and I walk as though I am going straight to the bathroom but then detour over to Greg's table.

"Hi, Greg," I say as I sit down across from him. Out of the corner of my eye I can see Tess turn cherry Tootsie Pop red.

"Hey. What's up?" We don't talk about our night at Lisa's. What would be the point?

"Not much. Just tired of studying. Tess and I have a big test tomorrow."

"What subject?"

"Science. We're both awful." This is a huge lie. Tess could teach our class if she wanted to. "Want to come tutor us?"

Greg closes his textbook and gives me a small smile. "Yeah, no problem."

"Great! We're sitting over there." I point to Tess. "I'm just going to go to the bathroom."

I smile at him before I walk away, planning to leave them alone for the rest of the period. Sometimes people just need a good kick in the pants. Myself included. I go to the back rows of the library, looking for a decent book to check out. I notice Lisa in the row next to me, and I push some books on the shelf between us to the side. They fall all over the place.

"Sorry! I was trying to be smooth," I say.

Lisa shakes her head and keeps her attention on me.

"What do you want, Lei?"

"Nothing. I'm just giving my friend some alone time with a gentleman," I whisper.

"How noble of you," Lisa declares.

"How was the rest of your weekend?" I ask.

"Fine. But my mother yelled at me for not enjoying the festivities." Lisa rolls her eyes. "She told me she saw you at the party. Thanks for not telling her where I was."

I shove my hands in my pockets and kick at the carpet with my shoe. Lisa crosses her arms over her chest.

"You do realize we're talking to each other on school grounds," I point out.

She shrugs.

"Your friends won't mind?"

"I don't really give a shit."

"So I didn't get a part in the play. I'm just an under-study."

"That's understandable. Your gas is awful." She then stops my shoe with hers so I'll stop idly kicking the carpet. I do and look up to see Lisa grin at me.

FOURTEEN

After a week filled with a crappy science test, grueling play rehearsals, and listening to Tomas solidify our weekend plans for the millionth time, the day of our visit to Saskia's place arrives at last. I have had a few moments with Saskia here and there over the week, but she is constantly busy at play rehearsal, and I doubt she even notices me. And now, tonight is the night when I can talk to her as much as I want. Well, as much as Tomas lets me get a word in.

"I can't believe your friend lives here," Mom says as she drops me off in front of the Taj hotel in Boston.

"Thanks for the ride, Mom," I say before she can ask too many questions. I have no idea what's in store for this evening, but whatever it is, I am nervous.

"Call me when you need me to pick you up tomorrow."

"Uh-huh. Love you! Bye!" I close the door and jog inside to the lobby. I feel like a socialite going to meet her lover for a quick tryst before her husband comes home. How chic am I?

I knock on the penthouse door and Saskia opens it, beaming and hugging me. "You made it, Leila!" I am so blissfully happy.

"Wouldn't miss it." I take in the scent of her hair and my hormones are going bonkers, until Tomas yells my name and rushes toward me.

"Don't you just love this place?" He takes me by the arm and leads me to the kitchen area. "Can I make you a drink, young lady?"

"A drink?" I ask. Tomas begins to unscrew a bottle of Tanqueray, and I look at all the liquor around. I've never really had a drink before. There was a glass of champagne at a wedding once, but I had two sips and then decided it was gross.

"Uh . . . I don't know. Sure. Um . . . scotch?"

"Scotch! What are you, a forty-year-old man?" Tomas gives me a look like I'm from another planet. Or possibly a forty-year-old man.

"She'll have what I'm having. Two gin and tonics,

Tomas, if you would," Saskia says as though she's ordered drinks all her life. Tomas nods and begins to mix the drinks while Saskia links our arms and leads me to the couch.

"I am so glad you're here. This place just gets unbearable after a while." Saskia grins and pushes me down onto the sofa, playfully falling down next to me.

"I can't believe you live here!" I exclaim.

"It's not that glamorous, I'm afraid. You remember the story of Rapunzel? Trapped in a tower waiting for her prince to climb up her hair? Only in this case the tower is a hotel and the prince would probably hire someone to save me, saving himself the trouble."

I highly doubt that.

"I highly doubt that." Oh my God, I said it out loud!

"Sorry?"

"Well, you have hair Rapunzel would love to have, and I'm sure you don't need rescuing," I say as the word-vomit continues to spew out of my stupid mouth.

"Don't I? News to me." She smirks and I don't know what's happening. Are we having a moment? Is this a moment? She's just watching me, not looking away—and I'm not, either. I really, really should do something. Tomas rescues me, for once.

"Drinks are ready!"

I guzzle mine down. Tomas and Saskia laugh at my eagerness to consume alcohol. Turns out drinking's no big deal. It tastes just like Sprite with less sugar. I ask Tomas for another.

A little while later Tomas is online in the living room, chatting with God knows who, and Saskia and I wobble away into her room. I am totally coherent. Hahaha. Yeah. Totally . . . coherent. Those drinks were delicious! Delicious is a funny word. It should be spelled with an *I-S-H* like *wish* or *dish*! I wish for a dish!

"You can lie on the bed if you want," Saskia says. Bed! That's where sexy times happen! I'm not ready for sexy times! I flop on the bed and bury my face in the comforter. It's soft. I like it. I feel detached from myself and think about how good that feels, to not be me. I'm somebody, some*thing*, else entirely.

I hear Saskia's sweet voice. "Don't fall asleep, Leila. Our night's not over."

My face is still in the bed.

"It's not?" *It's not?*

"No, silly," she chirps like a Disney princess. "We're going out."

Oh. We're going out?

"Tomas has these friends at BU. We're going to hang

out with them. Tomas needs to meet some other men, and frankly high school parties are such a bore, don't you think?"

Are they? I haven't been to many of them.

"But how will we get there?" It's important to be practicaaaaaaaaaaaaaaaaal.

Saskia laughs at how ridiculous I am. She turns me over and stands above me.

"Cab. Metro. We'll figure it out." Her hair is falling into my face, tickling my nose. I hope I don't sneeze in her hair. "You're quite pretty when you're drunk," she says, and then turns and walks away. I feel like I'm losing my breath. I have to sober up, quick, even if I'm pretty. I'm pretty. I'm pretty. I'm pretty.

Soon we are on the T going to Boston University, and I keep trying to be less silly, but everything just makes me laugh. Tomas is laughing, too, but at me, and I just keep telling him to shut up. Saskia tells us to quiet down. I try to, but all these people are looking at us, and for the first time I really don't care. It's so freeing. I *want* them to look because I'm pretty. I'm pretty and young and alive. How about *that*, Vietnamese lady on the other side of the train? How about *that*, homeless guy leering at me from across the way? Tomas dances around the pole like he's a stripper, and Saskia stuffs dollars into his coat pockets. And I just laugh some more.

The cold air hits us as we get off the T. Saskia lights up two cigarettes in her mouth and passes one to Tomas. Tomas coughs as he takes a drag and Saskia winks at me when she exhales smoke. This night is epic and must never end! We link arms like in The *Wizard of Oz* and we shuffle off to Tomas's friends' house.

An hour into the party, I'm not having as much fun as I thought I would. Tomas is sucking face with some guy named Fred he met online, probably the guy he was talking to earlier. Saskia is talking to a guy named Chip about the ramifications of global warming. There are a few other people around, but none of them are talking to me and I keep staring at this poster of Che Guevara. I am comforted to know that I have less facial hair than he does. A girl with dreadlocks and a bullhorn in her nose sits next to me; we don't speak. She takes a hit from a penis-shaped bong, looks my way and offers it to me. I shake my head and say no thank you. She tells me her name's Rebecca and she's a gender studies major. I tell her my name's Leila and I'm undecided. This is the understatement of the year. I stopped drinking about an hour ago, and now I just feel sort of nauseated. Rebecca takes another hit and puts the penis-bong down on the table. Why is everything always about sex?

"Why is everything always about sex?" I say out loud. Rebecca grins, her eyes glazed over.

"What else is there to do sometimes, y'know?" I had assumed college students would be more articulate.

"Yeah, but it's everywhere, all the time. What's the big deal?" I ask.

"You haven't done it yet, right?" I'm so obviously a virgin. "Look, the first time is probably going to suck. It's like dancing, but there's no song. Your mom or whoever will say it's a special time in your life, but you still won't know what you're doing," Rebecca says, as if I asked for her advice.

I notice Saskia leaning in a little closer to Chip. Their conversation must be engaging.

"The second time is better. You get more comfortable with your body, and you start figuring out who and what you want. If you're lucky."

Chip is whispering something in Saskia's ear now. I didn't know the hole in the ozone layer required such intimacy.

"Then eventually, you get in bed with someone you just go wild on because you can't get enough of them. It's the best ever."

Chip kisses Saskia full on the mouth. I want to throw up.

"Where's the bathroom?" I ask.

Rebecca points me down the hall, and I walk past Saskia and Chip. Saskia's hand is on his chest, and his fingers are running through her hair. My stomach is hitting the floor. I close the bathroom door behind me. I grab the toilet seat and vomit. It's all the alcohol. I *want* it to be the alcohol. There's a knock on the door; I ignore it. Saskia barges in, and I hate having her see me like this. She closes the door behind her and crouches over me, making circles on my back with her hand.

"I shouldn't have let you drink so much," she murmurs.

I cry a little and wipe my mouth with toilet paper. "I'm sorry. I don't want you to have to miss the party."

"No, it's lame. College kids think they know everything."

Eventually I think I don't have anything left to heave. I just sit there, unable to look her in the eye.

"I remember when I had too much to drink for the first time," Saskia says. "My daddy was hosting a party and was too busy to notice that I was having a lousy evening. The bartender left the bar area for a while, and I snuck some peppermint schnapps, of all things. Needless to say, I have never been able to eat a York Peppermint Pattie since."

"I'm sorry," I whisper.

"You really should learn to stop apologizing, especially when things aren't your fault."

I wipe my eyes with the back of my hands. This is hardly charming or flirtatious. This is just sad and pathetic.

"Anyway, I was twelve and I ended up spending the whole night in the bathroom. Eventually Daddy came to say good night. I told him I ate some bad shrimp or something and he believed me. Or he pretended to," she says.

I take her hand in mine. "Thanks for not leaving me alone." I say.

Saskia smiles and squeezes my hand. "I wouldn't think of it."

After a while I get my bearings and we pry Tomas away from Fred. Rebecca is making out with some other girl. The three of us link arms and take a cab back to the hotel.

Tomas passes out on the couch. He's had a great evening, that's for sure. I'm pretty sober now, but Saskia still holds my hand and leads me to her bathroom.

"The nice thing about living in a hotel is all the extra toiletries," Saskia says, taking out a toothbrush for me. I brush my teeth while she brushes her hair.

"Was Chip a good kisser?" I ask, like I'm a gal pal rather than a hopeful love interest.

"Not really," she says with a sigh. "I was just kind of bored. I stopped it after a while."

"Do you think you'll see him again?"

She laughs at my question. "God no. A guy by the name of Chip is not exactly the prince I was hoping would come to rescue me from my tower. Besides, he didn't know all that much about fracking." She puts her hairbrush down and rubs my back again. "Let's go to bed, okay?" She walks away and I rinse my mouth.

Saskia sits in her bed, getting comfortable. I stand at the end of the bed.

"So I'm just going to go sleep on a couch," I say.

"Nonsense. You're coming in here with me."

I am? "I don't know. I mean, is there enough room? I might kick in my sleep or something."

"Leila, I want you to," she says.

I pull back the sheets and get under the covers as Saskia turns off her bedside lamp. This is no big deal. We're friends. I lie down next to her, rigid. This is no big deal.

"Did it bother you? Watching me with him?" Saskia asks in the darkness.

How do I answer that?

"Yes."

She puts an arm around me and pulls me in closer.

"Don't worry. We'll find you a boy to kiss soon, too."

Right. A boy.

She closes her eyes and I end up sleeping about twenty minutes the entire night.

FIFTEEN

It's a new day at school and Ashley is sitting in Robert's lap on an alcove bench, marking her territory like a conquistador with a flag to plant. Apparently things heated up between them at Lisa's party after Greg and I left. Already I'm sick of them together. I'm not heterophobic or anything. I just wish I didn't have to watch them express their lust for each other *all* the time.

Ashley twirls a lollipop in her mouth, and I see Mr. Carr out of the corner of my eye, quickening his step down the hallway, clearly pretending not to see them. Mr. Carr has never been good at dealing with teenage hormones. He never wants to chaperone dances and have to break up dirty dancing.

"Hey, Leila." Greg walks over to the bench I'm sitting on, and I'm relieved to have someone to commiserate with. "What's going on there?"

"I guess she's moved on from Mr. Harris."

"Don't tell me you believe that rumor?" Greg says as he continues to watch the new couple. "You just hate science class. He's not so bad. Wow. If Ashley ever becomes broke she could sure work as a stripper."

"Study up on strippers much?" He blushes and I don't know why I said that. It was supposed to be funny, but obviously it challenges his manhood or something. "I'm going to study with Tess again if you want to join us."

He raises an eyebrow at me and folds his arms. "Tess didn't need any help at all. In fact I think she wrote the textbook under a pen name, she knew the material so well."

"I thought you might be good study buddies!"

He looks down at his shoes for a minute before making direct eye contact with me. "I get that you and me aren't going to happen, but you don't have to pawn me off to your friend." Why did I ever try my hand at matchmaking? And I thought we were over talking about the prospect of "us."

"That wasn't why I . . . Tess is cool and so are you and I thought—"

He cuts me off. "I'm sure Tess is cool, but just let me figure that out in my own time, okay?"

I stand up and look him right in the eye. "I will stay out of that department. I swear on our copy of *Zombie Killers Part II*." It's the best installment of the Zombie Killers franchise, at least as far as Greg and I are concerned. This loosens him up and he relaxes his shoulders. I extend my hand for him to shake. He laughs and shakes my hand firmly.

"Well, what have we here?" I hear Saskia's voice a moment before I feel the sting of her smack against my butt. I shriek in surprise and she laughs at my reaction. "Leila, it's just me."

"Sorry, I'm just a little jumpy today." And every day when you grab my ass.

"It must be Greg's effect on you. And I can see why." Saskia winks at Greg and he blushes. "Are you two going out this weekend?"

"No!" I say more adamantly than I should. "I don't have any weekend plans yet."

"We'll have to remedy that then, won't we, Greg?" Greg blinks at Saskia like he's just seen a meteor shower. She really is that breathtaking up close. Saskia links her arm in mine and drags me away from the school hallways.

"Where are we going?" I ask.

"We're pulling a Ferris." A what? Saskia leads us out to the parking lot, a sly grin on her face, and unlocks the door to her brand-new BMW.

"I've got a science test! And we have play rehearsal," I protest.

"You worry so much, Leila! You're going to get frown lines." Saskia looks out toward the bleachers at the side of the parking lot and rolls down her window. "What's your friend's name over there? The one smoking?"

I look and see Lisa, alone and staring out at the empty concrete.

"Lisa Katz."

"Yoo-hoo! Lisa! " Saskia waves Lisa over. Lisa puts out her cigarette and jogs over to the car. "I'm sorry to bother you, but do you have an extra cigarette?"

Lisa fumbles in her coat pocket for her box of Marlboro Menthols.

Saskia giggles. "How can you smoke these? They're so minty!" She brings out a Zippo lighter engraved with her initials. "Lisa, what are you doing now?"

Moments later Saskia and I sit in the front of the car, Lisa sits in the back, and Saskia has the windows down. The wind and smoke blow in my face. We're driving into downtown Boston and part of me feels intoxicated with a newfound feeling of rebellion; part of me is just freezing in the wind. Saskia and Lisa are talking about Monte Carlo and how they both find it to be very overrated. I just look out the window and hope Saskia will turn on the heat at some point.

"You're awfully quiet, Leila. Not having fun?" Saskia asks as she flicks her cigarette out the window and changes the radio station.

"No, I'm having fun. Just a little cold, I guess." Lisa throws out her half-smoked cigarette and rolls up her window while Saskia continues to fiddle with the radio, wind blowing through her hair.

When we get to Forever 21, Saskia is on a mission to find me a perfect bra, and she insists on paying for it. The saleswomen at Forever 21 seem to know Saskia pretty well and show her different colors and patterns while Lisa and I stand awkwardly to the side.

"Why does she care so much about your boobs?" Lisa says, flicking the tags hanging from clothes on a nearby rack.

"I don't know. She just likes doing stuff like this, I guess. She's always up for adventure, you know?"

"I hardly call hanging around boutiques on Newbury Street an adventure."

"Yeah, but it's better than school."

Lisa shrugs in agreement as Saskia approaches us with three saleswomen in tow.

"We've found you a few options! Let's go try them on!"

I take the bras and walk into a dressing room, nearly closing the door on Saskia as she enters.

"After all that work, I'm certainly not going to wait outside!" Saskia says. "Take off your shirt and try the red one."

I just stare blankly at the red bra in my hand and then at Saskia.

"Oh, come on," she says playfully. "Don't be shy. It's nothing I haven't seen before. I have a pair, too. Not as big as yours of course, but same idea."

I turn my body into one corner, my back toward Saskia, take off my shirt, and unclasp my bra. I quickly throw the red straps over my shoulders, fiddling with the back hooks. Saskia's hands touch mine and she does my bra for me, her fingers making tracings on my back. I might die if I hold my breath any longer.

"You should really do something about the blemishes on your back. I have a cream I can lend you." Thanks? I would be offended if I wasn't so nervous about how close she is. She swings my body around and backs away from me, inspecting me in the bra. I cover my stomach with my arms and hope this won't last much longer. Saskia opens the dressing room door and motions for me to come to the doorway.

"What do you think of this one?" Saskia asks the three salesladies as she nudges me into the hallway of the fitting area. Oh my God. Talk about mortifying. Lisa looks at the ceiling, probably embarrassed for me.

The salesladies scrutinize my body as I worry about what they must be thinking. My face is already scorching when a little girl walking past the dressing rooms yells out, "Mommy! Her boobs are huge!" The mommy hushes the girl up, and the saleslady suggests with a fake European accent that I should try on a bigger size. Saskia asks for a few more bras and pulls me into the dressing room.

"Don't be embarrassed," she says, holding my face in her hands. "I'm jealous of your boobs! They just scream sexy." She kisses me on the cheek and my mood lightens immediately.

I find one that works in the next batch. At last the humiliation is over. I thank Saskia for the bra she bought me. I fold my arms over my chest for the rest of our walk on Newbury Street, during which Saskia buys herself a clutch at a price that I'd rather not think about. Lisa manipulates mannequin arms into lewd positions whenever she has the chance.

"Don't you just love shopping?" Saskia asks, swaying her shopping bag from side to side.

"It's cool," I say, and Lisa gives me a look. She definitely remembers how much I hated clothes shopping with my mom when we were younger.

"How about we go somewhere else?" Lisa suggests. "Want to check out the aquarium?" I will have to remember to thank her later.

I haven't been to the New England Aquarium in years, but it's just as I remembered it. The inside of the building is dark, with the blue illuminations of the tank brightening the faces of the little kids who are plastered against the glass, trying to spot fish their friends haven't seen yet.

"It smells like fish in here," Saskia says, gazing past her reflection at a tiger shark.

"What else would it smell like? It's an aquarium," I manage while making blowfish faces through the glass.

"Still, you'd think they'd be able to do something about that. Maybe a few air fresheners." She crinkles her nose at the smell, and then nods her head toward Lisa, who is over at the railing, looking down at the penguins. "She's an odd one, isn't she?" Saskia asks.

"No, she's just going through some stuff right now."

"Who isn't? We're supposed to. It's that coming-of-age

thing, right? I'm going to have a cigarette. Let me know if the fish do anything other than swim around in circles." I watch Saskia walk away and make my way over to Lisa.

"Are you a penguin fan?" Lisa asks as I stand next to her.

"Of course," I admit like a nerd. "They don't restrict themselves to gender roles, you know."

"How's that?"

"Well, the female emperor penguin lays the egg, but the male has to sit on it, waiting for it to hatch while the female goes off to forage for food. Very progressive."

"Huh. I just like them because they run like you do," she says with a straight face. The penguins waddle off the rocks and into the water. When the last one glides under the surface, Lisa turns to face me. "Thanks for today, Lei. I really couldn't deal with school."

It's good hearing Lisa talk about her feelings. I press my luck. I don't know why, maybe it's just curiosity or a guilty feeling that I haven't been a better friend, even if it was she who pushed me away. "How are you, Lisa? Really?"

Lisa gnaws on her lower lip. "I feel like I can't handle anything. But I can't . . . I don't want to talk about it. Not today."

I try to remember what I used to say to make her feel better when we were kids, but it feels like forever ago. "Don't thank me for today. It was Saskia's idea. I should be thanking *you*. If it were up to her we'd be shopping all day."

Lisa stops worrying her lip and is back to her stoic self. "Yeah, that was annoying," she says. "What's her deal?"

That's weird. I thought they were getting along.

"You don't like shopping? Won't Ashley be upset if she finds you've changed your tune?"

"I don't really hang out with Ashley's group much outside of school. They're kind of mean," she admits, pulling on her bangs.

"You think?"

She flashes me a smile. "Okay, okay. I guess I just never noticed it before. Or maybe I did, but then I figured out that being mean is kind of exhausting."

"Ashley must be really tired then."

"Oh, she'll be fine. She snorts Adderall, so she has loads of energy."

"Jeez."

"Yeah. She thinks it's cool or whatever, but she ends up getting blue boogers. Still, she says when she's on it she and her boyfriends mate like rabbits." The penguins are back on the rocks, waddling around, bumping into one another and jabbering and yelling over one another. "They look like high school students," Lisa says.

"Want to go see the sea turtle?" I ask. "It just swims around and around, but I love it."

Lisa smiles and we walk up the ramp to the top of the tank.

We drive back to school and some new pop star's song full of sexual innuendo comes on the radio.

"Ahh! I love this song!" Saskia screams. Lisa flicks her cigarette out the window and they both start to sing. I'm in the backseat this time, where I can I sit back and watch them fling their hair and mock the sexy dance moves from the video. They're both pretty and free, and I'm almost in awe of them.

As we pull into the school parking lot, I notice my mom's car parked crookedly in a handicapped spot up front. Busted.

Mom doesn't speak to me on the way home. She drives slowly, and I don't dare look at her because then I'll see that her jaw is still clenched and that the vein in her forehead looks like the Amazon River. When the school called her to see if I had left early, she panicked and called my cell phone thirteen times. Of course, I'd left my cell phone in my locker and didn't think to get it when Saskia whisked me away. Unable to find me, my mother called the police, but they informed her it wasn't a missing person's case since I'd only been gone for three hours. They told her I was probably cutting class, which she didn't like one bit. Back at school she tracked down as many kids and teachers as she could think of who might know something, including Mr. Carr, Tess, Greg, Ms. Taylor, and Mr. Harris, who informed her that I missed an important test. Always helping out the kids, Mr. Harris.

When we got back to school, everyone breathed with relief—and then they freaked out. Mr. Carr told Lisa her mom was deeply upset but couldn't be there since she had a pilates class. Saskia's parents were in Prague or some-where. I don't even think they were contacted. No wonder Saskia didn't care about ditching school—she's the only one who couldn't get in trouble with her parents. And you know what? This new bra is too tight.

"I just don't know what you're thinking anymore," Mom says as I stare at the floor mat of her Mercedes. Its crev-ices are filled with sand and dirt, and I feel like I should be there with it. "You used to tell me everything. And now you don't tell me anything. It's like you . . . I don't know. I don't know who you are. I don't know what's upset you."

"Sorry." And I was. And this time it was definitely my fault.

When Dad got home, Mom surprised me by not mentioning anything about my skipping school to him. I don't know why not. Maybe she didn't want him to freak out, or maybe she was just doing me a favor, but it seems like a hopeful sign. I'm not ready to make any sudden confessions to her, but it's good to know that there are things about me my mother doesn't necessarily feel she has to share with my dad.

SIXTEEN

Mr. Harris didn't let me make up the test. He is now giving me a D as my midsemester grade. Ms. Taylor's been out of school for two days. She hardly ever uses her sick days, so I assume it has to do with Mr. Harris, and is possibly contributing to his bad mood. I haven't told my parents about the grade, since I'm already walking on eggshells around my mom, and my dad's always griping about Armstead tuition. I can't let him think that I'm wasting his money. Now I have to get a B on the next few tests, or I'm toast. But I really doubt it's going to happen.

The play is taking up a lot of time. It's been fun so far, when I'm not mooning over Saskia, and I'm learning a lot about the technical aspects of production from Taryn and her crew. Despite their icy exteriors they've been pretty welcoming, doing things like offering to lend me graphic novels they think I'd like. We spend a lot of time in the booth overlooking the stage, and it's surprisingly fun.

"Check this out," Taryn says one afternoon as she plays Pink Floyd's "Money" on the auditorium speakers. She's set up lighting cues to create a psychedelic show onstage in time with the music.

"That's awesome!" I say, and I really truly mean it. When the spectacle is over, Taryn drinks from her flask and I work on the lighting cues for the play. Christina sleeps on the couch until it's time to leave, as usual. Simone is working on knitting a purse, but I don't quite see it yet. She's in charge of costumes and props, so she has a lot downtime. She's even teaching me to crochet.

The most surprising thing about the production is how good an actress Tess is. When she's in character, she commits herself fully to it. It's just the way she is with her schoolwork. Sometimes when she's not onstage, she helps me with my science homework. And by that I mean she does it for me while I pretend that I understand what she's doing.

Tomas is still Tomas, relentlessly flirting with a senior

who's playing Orsino, but I don't think the senior understands that Tomas is flirting with him. In any case it's kept Tomas out of my hair. Saskia has been brilliant, of course, and sometimes I think she must be bored with being so perfect at everything. She and I have been hanging out a lot lately. We walk to class and rehearsal together with our arms joined at the elbow and have inside jokes, though sometimes they are at our classmates' expense. I imagine this is how Europeans behave, very touchy-feely without it really meaning anything. Still, I like to pretend it's also what having a girlfriend might be like. Not that my imagination always stops there.

"Christina! Wake up!" Taryn shouts while building a platform.

Christina's head rises, and she looks disoriented. "Where'd you put the hacksaw? I can't find it anywhere." Christina points to a shelf up high and lays her head back down, going to sleep.

"Worst tech crew ever," Taryn mutters.

"She's just nervous about the show coming up so soon," Simone says, coils of yarn piled at her feet. "I was thinking we could get some dry ice for a fog effect."

"Yeah, let's add another stupid errand to the ever-growing list," Taryn says while she measures wood with a ruler.

"You know, Taryn, you've been such a bitch since the PETA petition," Simone snaps back. "So we didn't get enough signatures. We will next time."

They argue some more. I leave them to it while I watch the stage. Saskia circles Tess with a kind of predatory look. Is that part of her character?

"Stop drooling over her," Taryn says, coming over to me. I glare at her, but mostly I'm embarrassed.

"It's all right, Leila," Simone says, smiling at me as she joins us. "We don't judge here." I'm totally blushing now and glance at the floor.

"Am I that obvious?" I say meekly. Christina has miraculously woken up and appeared like the vampire she pretends to be. She pats my shoulder.

"We've all seen this play forty times. Yet you always pay attention to Saskia's scenes. Every. Time. It's kind of hard not to notice," Christina says.

"No, I mean, do I look . . . do I look gay?" They all laugh at me. "Well, you guys have the look down," I mumble. They all stare at one another. Then Taryn shakes her head, Simone looks at me like I am speaking a new language for the first time, and Christina yawns.

"Sorry, did I—I didn't mean to offend you."

"Wow. Um, you've got a lot to learn," says Taryn, sawing into some wood.

"We're not gay," Simone says. I look at the three of them, my gaze landing on Taryn's shaved head.

"Wait? What?" I say, flabbergasted. "You're kidding, right?"

"We're not gay," Taryn repeats, matter-of-factly. "My boyfriend goes to public school, Simone just has the hobbies of her grandma, and Christina's into the undead, so that kind of limits her dating options." I start to sweat.

"Oh my God." I cover my face with my hands. It was one thing when I thought I was confiding to "my people," but I'm left with the scary realization that I'm alone—and exposed.

"Hey, it's okay. There's no reason to be ashamed!" Simone says, coming to my side. "I've got two moms and I love them both. I know tons of gay people and they have well-adjusted lives. Well, except for Uncle Bill. He has those larceny charges . . . But otherwise there's nothing to worry about."

My hands are still over my face. I'm not ready to look at any of them yet.

"We won't tell anyone. Right, girls?" says Simone.

"Christ, since when did tech crew turn into the Oprah

show?" says Taryn. "Look, Leila, high school sucks for everybody. We know what that's like, so we're not going to say anything." I uncover my face and look at the group.

"There are a lot of gay vampires," Christina says with a shrug. I suppose that's her idea of comforting.

"Thanks. I just haven't figured it all out yet. Maybe it's just a phase," I say timidly.

"Sure," Taryn says, rolling her eyes. "A phase."

"Can we talk about something else, please?" I beseech them.

"Well, whatever you're going through, it's cool with us," Christina says. The girls nod and we go back to work. I like keeping busy and focusing on the task at hand. I feel like I have people I can talk to, and that's more than I ever thought I would get out of stage-managing.

"Do you know this music?" Saskia asks as I sit on her sofa, listening to the odd singing with a smooth background. She invited me over to her house after rehearsal. Her parents are out to dinner with friends. I had to call and beg my mom after the whole skipping school fiasco, but she acquiesced when I told her Tess would be there and we would study. Tess isn't here, of course. Yes, I lied. "It's the Ethiopiques.

Afro jazz from a while ago. Who knows what they're saying, but it sounds great, doesn't it?"

I nod and keep sipping the wine Saskia has poured for us. We're sitting a few feet apart.

"I'm so nervous for the play," Saskia goes on. "Everyone seems fairly well-prepared. It's just that something about Tess playing Cesario puts me off."

"Oh?" I say, sipping my wine, trying to look sophisticated, though I can feel that my cheeks are as red as a bag of Twizzlers.

"I don't know what it is. She just has no personality and tries so hard. I'd encourage her to take private acting lessons, but she probably couldn't afford it." It's quiet for a moment while I pretend she didn't say what she did.

"I think you would have made a great Cesario, Leila. Too bad Tess didn't get sick or anything," Saskia says.

"I think she's doing a pretty good job."

"But it's so hard to pretend to fall in love with her. If *you* were in the part I'd have no trouble at all."

I look at Saskia wide-eyed and she radiates. She's probably just being friendly.

"More wine?" she asks. I nod and she pours me another glass.

"Is Tomas coming?" I ask, kind of hoping he is so I can stop feeling so nervous.

"No. I thought we'd just have a girls' night this time."

What is happening?

"You've been such a good friend lately. I want to hear about what's going on in your life," she says.

"I'm, um . . . I'm failing science."

"You'll be fine. I'm sure we can find test answers for you. Or we can blackmail Mr. Harris. Or seduce him. He is cute. I'm sure it wouldn't be too difficult."

I stare at her in disbelief.

"Oh, I'm kidding. You should see your face. You take everything so literally." Saskia turns on the TV and flips through the channels. "Do you want to order an adult movie?"

No, really, what is happening? "No, I'm good, thanks," I say before sipping some more wine.

"You don't like sex?"

I laugh nervously. She's so blunt. I'm not sure if that's a European thing or the wine. "You know Greg likes you. I can tell," she says.

"We're just friends," I say, staring at the carpet.

"He just doesn't do it for you. I understand." Saskia

turns off the TV. "It's so boring up here. Do you want food or anything?"

"I'm not very hungry."

"So you're definitely not interested in Greg?" she asks.

"No. I'm not."

Saskia leans in closer as she puts her glass on the table. Her breath smells of wine. "Then who are you interested in?" she asks calmly, scanning my face. I stare at her in shock, clutching my glass. Is she suggesting what I think she is? She smiles and says, "Well, go on and kiss me. I don't mind."

I let out a nervous squeak and Saskia laughs. She takes the glass from my hand and puts it on the table. "We'll keep it between us, yeah?" she says, and I nod, dazed. She leans in and kisses me, tentatively at first, and I tremble a little before I respond. I close my eyes and try to lose myself in the kiss. Saskia makes me forget almost everything as she claims my mouth.

Wow.

I back away and she smiles sweetly. "Should we try again?" I don't really know how to answer her, so I nod once more and she takes the lead again, slowing her pace. Just as I am hoping we can do this for hours, she breaks away.

Laughing, she holds her hand up for a high five. "We are awesome!"

Um. Okay.

"Was I your first girl kiss?" she asks slyly.

I almost want to lie to her so she doesn't feel disappointed. "No. There was someone over the summer," I say. I can't stop staring at her lips.

She bites her bottom lip. "Was she prettier than me?" Seriously?

"No. There's no one prettier than you," I admit. Anastasia was adorable, but no one I've met before has Saskia's supermodel good looks.

"Was she better at kissing than I was?" I don't know why she's asking, but I'm willing to risk a bold answer. I lean in to kiss her this time and she moans. I nearly die.

"No," I answer at last. That isn't exactly true, because nothing can really compete with the feeling of a first kiss ... but I'm pretty sure an entire garden of Georgia O'Keeffe flowers has bloomed to life in my chest.

SEVENTEEN

When Ms. Taylor comes back to school I'm glad, because I thought I would finally have someone to talk to about my lurid encounter with Saskia. Only I was right, she and Mr. Harris have broken up. She doesn't say so explicitly, but in all her classes she's really upset and gets weepy about totally mundane things. We started reading *The Scarlet Letter*.

"So Hester has to wear a scarlet *A* because she commits the sin of adultery. But there aren't any men wearing something to show their sins. I mean, let's say a man said he was ready to take the next step in a relationship and then backed out because he felt 'overwhelmed.' That man should then wear a scarlet *C* for cowardice, don't you think?" No one can look away from Ms. Taylor as she rants.

Ashley mouths the word *crazy* to Robert, and Ms. Taylor must see her. Ms. Taylor's eye twitches and she walks over to Ashley. Ashley shrinks in her seat a little.

"Ashley, with all of your gifts of perception, I'm surprised you weren't able to find all the grammatical errors in your paper." Lisa and I look at each other. Maybe the Mr. Harris/Ashley affair is more than just a rumor after all.

Ms. Taylor walks back to her desk. "No homework tonight. You guys can go." The class files out. Robert doesn't even wait for the door to close before he starts laughing hysterically. I linger behind and approach Ms. Taylor's desk.

"Do you need anything?" I ask.

"Oh, no Leila, thank you. You're very sweet. I guess I made a fool of myself today."

"I don't think anyone noticed," I lie, giving her shoulder a light pat. Ms. Taylor begins to cry, and I really don't know what to do. She wipes her eyes.

"I'm sorry, Leila, this is completely unprofessional. God, you're so lucky you're a lesbian."

I panic, looking around just to double-check that, yes, we're still the only two left in the classroom. Ms. Taylor takes a deep breath and blinks a few times.

"I think I'm dating a girl," I whisper. She blinks and smiles.

"Oh, that's nice! Good for you! I'm happy to hear it."

"Thanks. And hey, you can do way better than Mr. Harris. He's lame." She shakes her head and puts her hands up.

"No, Leila, that's sweet but you don't have to take sides. He's your teacher, too, and a respected member of the community, even though he's confused about some things. Like what he looks for in a woman. Or whether he wants to have kids one day. But he's a good man.

I nod.

"Are you still doing poorly in his class?"

I nod again.

"Well, study harder. Put your best foot forward and all that," she says.

I smile and we both enter an awkward silence.

"I think I'm going to go to the nurse's office," Ms. Taylor finally says.

I head out the door.

There's still time left in the class period and almost everyone from my English class is hanging around the hallway, gossiping about our once-mighty but now-fallen teacher. Lisa sits on a bench by herself and I sit down next to her.

"Is Ms. Taylor okay?" Lisa asks.

"I think so."

"I guess she broke up with someone."

"What tipped you off, Katz?" We both smile and she kicks my shoe with hers.

"How's the play?"

"Almost over. You coming to the show?"

She shrugs.

"I'll take that as a maybe."

EIGHTEEN

In spite of what I told Ms. Taylor, Saskia's barely talked to me this week, since our kiss. I would ask her what her problem is, but I want to keep things cool. I don't want to seem needy, clingy, or insecure—even though I am. I caught up with her backstage before a tech rehearsal, mostly to double-check her last-minute blocking.

"Hey, Saskia, I just wanted to go over where the lights are going to be hitting you." She grins and pulls me into her.

"I'm sorry I haven't seen you lately," she says. "I've been so busy." I look around and make sure no one is watching. "I've decided to have a party at my place once the play is over. You can sleep over if you want."

I hold on to my clipboard tightly. "Okay, yeah, that'd be cool."

She smiles and tilts her head to the left, looking me over. "It's a shame we couldn't work together onstage. I'd have loved to act with you."

"Me too," I say before Tomas walks by. He raises his eyebrows and smirks while I quickly pull away from Saskia.

"Ladies, am I interrupting?"

"We're just running lines, sweetie," says Saskia, playing with the microphone on my headset. "See you two later." Saskia skips out in her Shakespearean frock and I bite my lip, looking down at the stage. Tomas smiles and walks over to me.

"So. A lesbian, huh? I'm kind of grossed out but intrigued."

"I'm not—"

"Uh-huh. It's always the quiet ones."

"Look, if you say anything,"

"Relax. Secret's safe and all that. Though if you came out, it wouldn't be that big a deal. You girls have it way easier."

My mouth opens in shock.

"Two hot girls in high school? No problem, definitely encouraged by my straight male counterparts. However a gay guy—even one as handsome as myself? Not as cool. Double standards. High school breeds them. God, I can't wait until college."

I sit down on the stage ramp. "My parents don't know," I say. Tomas looks at me sympathetically.

"That's a tough one."

"How did your parents react?"

"Well, my mother cried for a month. She went on about the grandkids she wouldn't have, and why couldn't this have happened to her sister's kids. I think my dad sort of knew for a while. He got me tickets to see *Wicked* last year. They aren't crazy about it, but they got over it."

"Yeah, but your parents aren't from Iran."

"No, but they're uptight WASPs who have reputations at the country club. It's just as difficult." Tomas smiles and extends his hand down to me and tries to pull me up. "God, you weigh a ton."

"I do not! I'm a decent size!"

"Okay, fatty." He smiles and pinches my cheek. "Did we just gay-bond right now?"

I go to the booth and sit down beside Taryn. Christina is on the couch, sleeping.

"What are you so happy about?" Taryn asks.

"I just feel good, that's all."

"Uh-huh." Taryn says. I can almost hear her eyes rolling.

I set up the cues. The lights go down and we're ready to go.

It is finally the day of the play. Mom hands me a granola bar and says she'll see me at the show. We kiss each other good-bye while Dad waits in the car, his NPR blasting. I hop in and he smiles.

"So the play is tonight?" Dad asks as though Mom hasn't reminded him twenty times.

"Yeah. You don't have to come—I'm backstage and everything."

"I'll try and make it. I'll see how my schedule goes today." There's a news story about Iran–United States relations, and Dad turns up the volume. He's been here for so many years, yet he still loves to be in the know about his former country. Iran's like an ex-lover he can't shake even though he's fairly content with his wife, America.

Dad listens to world events while I think about Saskia and the after-party. She asked me to sleep over, but . . . is she going to expect more than kissing? I don't know if I'm ready for that. I don't even know what to do! Should I pick up a manual or something?

"What has you so preoccupied, Leila *joon*?"

"Nothing! Nothing," I say nervously.

"When this play's finally over, maybe you can get back to studying?"

"Sure, Dad."

"Good. You can't be a doctor without a good feel for science. It just won't work." I want to bash my head on the dashboard. He still has hopes for me following in his footsteps, even though I've repeatedly said medicine isn't for me. At least he has Nahal.

We pull up to the front entrance of the school and there's Lisa, walking from her car. Dad puts the window down.

"Hi, Lisa! How are you?" he calls. Lisa turns and smiles.

"Hi, Dr. Azadi. I'm fine, thanks."

"Haven't seen you in a long time! Come by the house. My wife would love to cook eggplant stew for you!" I'm impressed that Dad remembers Lisa loved it when Mom made it. Lisa smiles again and waits for me while I exit the car, slamming the door behind me. Dad waves good-bye to us both and drives away.

"He loves you," I tell Lisa. "You always call him *Doctor* instead of *Mister*."

"Well, he earned those degrees, Mash'Allah!" Lisa says in faux seriousness. I raise my eyebrows in shock that she remembered a phrase that expresses joy and gratitude, and that she's joking around. "Don't get used to it. I'm still sad, angry, and depressed most days. Guess you just bring out my sunny side." She gives me another small smile.

Lucky me. Greg walks up to us and does a double-take. He seems surprised to see Lisa speaking with me. "Hey, Leila, you ready for the show tonight?" he asks.

"I guess. Everyone's worked pretty hard."

"Cool. Well, break a leg," he says before he dashes off to some of his guy friends. Lisa and I continue to walk toward the school.

"He's still kind of in love with you," Lisa says.

"We're just friends."

"So you've said. I don't see it, either, but I guess he could grow on you. Like a tumor." Lisa and I laugh and we walk by Ashley and her gang, sitting in the small alcove. I'll leave her to her group, but getting Lisa to loosen up feels like a huge victory.

NINETEEN

The show goes fantastically. The audiences for the first two performances are wowed. Taryn's lighting cues really look like a thunderstorm. The dry ice Simone suggested gives a nice fog effect when Tess lies onstage in a tattered dress, as though she has really washed ashore. The Illyria set is designed to look like a modern-day mansion. The wings of the stage are painted to look like the seashore, with blue fabric billowing from the breeze of a small fan nearby. All the actors are dressed in modern clothing, but they are speaking in Shakespearean English. We figured it'd be more relatable to our peers, or at least, fewer people would fall asleep.

The third and final night, we have our biggest audience—a full house. Tess is doing her usual incredible job of pretending to be a man and speaking with Orsino. Tonight, though, she looks a little sweaty, even from up in the lighting booth. But things are going fine, or so I think until my headset crackles to life, and I hear Tomas freaking out. "Leila! Leila! Oh God!"

"What is it?" I ask, hoping Tomas is panicking about something stupid, like a cute boy being in the audience.

"It's Tess! She's really sick! Mr. Kessler is back here with her! She's throwing up in a bucket! What do we do?"

Before I can answer, Mr. Kessler has grabbed Tomas's headset. "Know all your lines, Leila? 'Cause you're on. Let Taryn take over, and you come here as quickly and as quietly as possible."

He's having me fill her role! I am her understudy, after all, though I am terrified and hope to God I remember half my lines. I take off my headset and fling it on the light board.

"Something's wrong with Tess! They need me back-stage! Christina, wake up!" The vampire girl sleeping on the couch behind us continues to snore. "CHRISTINA! WAKE UP!"

Christina sits up, blinking, and yells a little. I drag her over to my stool at the light board and plop the headset on.

"Christina, all the notes for the light changes are marked in this script. Taryn knows what to do, but you need to guide her, okay? I'll buy you a pair of fangs if you don't mess this up."

Taryn gives me a nod of approval, and I quietly exit the booth, trying not to disturb the audience as I find my way backstage.

When I get there, Tomas throws a costume in my face. "You'd better get dressed. You go on in a couple minutes." He starts to fuss with my hair.

I see Saskia onstage, proudly acting her part, and know the audience is eating it up. Then I see Tess, hunched over in the corner, pale and glistening with sweat. I put on my costume in a hurry, and Mr. Kessler comes over to deliver his version of a pep talk.

"Well, Leila, this is unexpected. But life is like that sometimes and I see this as a good time to build character. Like when I got fired and I saw it as an opportunity to pursue my love of bluegrass and started a band. Granted, the band didn't go anywhere, but still, lots of fun! So let's look at this as a positive experience!" I nod nervously while Tomas puts a false mustache on my upper lip.

"All right," he says. "No pressure or anything, but this show is depending on you now. It's just a high school play. No big deal. But, you know, you're the *lead*. You do know your lines, right?" I nod again.

"All right, you're up. Try not to fart out there," Mr. Kessler says with a chuckle.

He really couldn't be more inspirational. "I'll do my best." I take one last look at Tess, who gives me a weak smile before throwing up in the bucket again. I smile back sympathetically, and Tomas pushes me onstage.

I stumble as I make my entrance. I see the Carrs looking confused and whispering about what could have happened to Tess. My family's in the audience, too. Mom makes a little clapping motion, and my dad is smiling widely. Nahal edges to the front of her seat and films me on her phone. I look to my left and see Saskia. My throat catches as she gives me a sly smirk.

I deliver my first line. "The honorable lady of the house, which is she?"

Saskia licks her lips before she answers. "Speak to me; I shall answer for her. Your will?" She raises her eyebrows and my mouth goes dry.

The auditorium is quiet for a few moments, and I can hear Tomas whispering lines to me. I think the entire audience can hear him. I have to keep going, and the next line comes from my mouth:

"Most radiant, exquisite and unmatchable beauty."

As the play continues I don't mess up too badly,

and all in the audience seem to be enjoying themselves. I definitely hear my dad laugh louder than he should, and I don't think he even really knows what is going on in the play, but God love him anyway. Soon I'm in another scene with Saskia, and her character, Olivia, is falling in love with my Cesario character. We have a good rhythm and chemistry going. That is, until she gets really, really close to me.

"Stay, I prithee, tell me what thou think'st of me." She takes my hand and my heart thumps a little louder.

"That you do think you are not what you are." I recite.

"If I think so, I think the same of you." She's giving me googly eyes. I don't really think she's acting now.

"Then think you right: I am not what I am."

I am not what I am. I am not what I am.

"I would you were as I would have you be!" And then she does it. In front of the whole audience, my parents, my uptight sister, the Carrs, Ms. Taylor, and the popular girls. She kisses me. It's a little peck, but I freak out because that is *definitely* not in the script. And then, it happens.

I go blank. I don't remember what to do or where to go. I can only blink at the audience in fright.

Tomas is yelling lines to me like I'm a first grader, which makes the audience laugh. When I break away, shocked, and run offstage, Saskia finishes the scene with delicious comic timing.

I shyly get through the rest of the play somehow. The audience is very kind and forgiving of my impromptu performance. At the end of the show Saskia takes my hand before we bow. As I rise from the bow, I see my parents standing and applauding. Ms. Taylor cheers; Tomas is in the wings, jumping up and down. I notice there's one person walking out of the auditorium already. It's Lisa Katz, but I'm sort of surprised she even came.

In the lobby my parents greet me and tell me I did a great job. The cast members chat and hug. Tomas is already talking to Mr. Kessler about the next season's production. Ms. Taylor congratulates me on my performance.

"You did a great job, Leila."

"Thanks, Ms. Taylor. I did my best, but obviously I didn't know I'd be going onstage."

"It's too bad about Tess. I know she was excited about her role. She looked like she wasn't feeling too well from the beginning of the evening. And I heard she was great in the first two performances." Ms. Taylor leans in a little closer and whispers to me. "Have a great night, superstar!" She grins, tousles my hair, and walks away.

Amid all the celebrating, I have to pee. In the bathroom

I find Saskia. She's wiped off all her stage makeup and is changing clothes out in the open. She's topless, about to put on a bra, but she doesn't bother to go into a stall.

"Hello, Viola! Wonderful performance tonight!" I turn my head away and she laughs at my bashful behavior.

"You did a good job tonight, Saskia. That kiss was unexpected."

"I thought I'd give you a surprise." Saskia grins as she opens up her tube of mascara. "You were so much better than Tess. She was such a ham the previous shows. We had no chemistry. I'd get lost staring at her acne instead of your gorgeous eyes." Saskia brushes her eyelashes with the mascara.

"Listen, I wish I could come to the party tonight, but I don't think I can. I don't really do well at parties," I say. "But you'll have plenty of fun with the whole cast and crew and everything."

"I didn't invite the whole cast. Certainly not the crew. God, can you imagine what conversations they'd start? How to drink human blood properly?"

"Those girls are actually pretty cool." I chuckle halfheartedly.

"You don't have feelings for them, do you?"

"What? No. They aren't even—"

She stops me with a kiss on my mouth. She's very good at this. I hear a door open and I back away. Lisa walks out of the farthest stall on the left. I cover my mouth with both my hands. I didn't know anyone was in here! I can't stand that I'm being caught out left and right.

Saskia stares at Lisa curiously. "Did you like the show?" she asks. It's not clear if she's referring to the play or to what just happened in the bathroom. Lisa washes her hands calmly, like she didn't hear a thing, then turns to us.

"I think you both gave a terrific performance." Just as Lisa's about to leave, Saskia invites her to the party. But Lisa goes out the door without responding.

TWENTY

Driving the four of us home, Dad has the BBC world news on at a low volume so he can keep complimenting me on the play. It's kind of nice seeing him and Mom so happy about something I've done, though Dad does mention that he wishes I were as good at science as I am at acting. Baby steps, I guess. Nahal has to ruin it by bringing up Tess Carr. She's always such a killjoy.

"Yeah, she got really sick all of a sudden. I feel bad for her," I say sincerely, hoping we can drop it and just talk about what a great job I did.

"She was pretty good at the beginning," says Nahal.

Yes, she was, Nahal. Why don't you fling yourself out of the car and hitchhike the rest of the way home?

"Her poor father looked so upset when he took her home," Mom says. "It's horrible when your babies get sick, even when they aren't babies anymore."

We drive in silence for a few minutes. No one brings up the kiss and I am grateful. Dad puts in a CD and everyone perks up again.

"Not this old Persian stuff!" Nahal gripes as Dad yells, rather than sings, the lyrics in Farsi. Mom covers her ears with her hands and Dad sings even more loudly.

When we get home, I mention Saskia's party. After that kiss, I really want to go. I can tell Mom's torn.

"Are her parents going to be there?" I don't want to lie to her. She must sense something in my hesitation. "I don't want you to go, Leila. There will be other parties. I promise, when your winter break starts you can have some friends over for pizza, okay?"

That sounds so lame. But whatever. This is only the party of a lifetime, celebrating my triumphant stage debut. No big deal. I can skip that.

Half an hour later I am pleading with Nahal to drive me to Saskia's party. I tell her I'll give her fifty bucks, but she just laughs in my face.

"Mom won't let you go, huh?"

I nod, feeling embarrassed that it has come to me pleading with my brownnoser sister.

"I used to make up stuff about going out, too. I'll tell Mom you're sleeping over with me. Go get ready, but leave your cute clothes in a bag and change in the car."

I'm impressed that Nahal is not only agreeing to this, but she's done this sort of thing before. So much for being the perfect daughter.

Nahal's excuse works like a charm. Of course. Mom thinks it's wonderful that we're bonding, and says she always knew this day would come. She gives me a big hug. I feel so guilty that I almost back out. Almost.

"I love you, Leila *joon*. See you tomorrow." Mom's not naive. I just don't think she'd ever expect Nahal to lie to her, or to lie for me for that matter.

"I love you, too, Mom," I say before I rush off to Nahal's car.

As soon as we get out of the driveway, Nahal puts on the heavy metal station. She stops the car and sticks a ring in her eyebrow. I don't know this person. She notices that I am gawking at her.

"What?"

I point at my eyebrow and point at her. She drives

again, fast, and not at all like she did when she lived at home. She shrugs.

"College. Let's keep it between us, okay?"

Nahal drops me off in front of the Taj. I've changed into my party clothes and feel pretty hot, if I do say so myself. "She's a rich bitch, huh?" Nahal asks. I didn't think Nahal even knew any swears. Something else she has hidden from our parents. I don't mention it, but all these secrets kind of make her more real.

"Do you have a ride home from the party?" sister dear asks.

"I'm going to sleep over."

Nahal nods.

"Nahal, how come you're being so cool about this?"

She shrugs. "I know Mom and Dad have high expectations. When I'm around them I try to meet them, but a person has to have a few secrets for herself." She pauses. "You know, Leila, I've actually always been jealous of you."

I look at her, shocked.

She laughs and continues. "I'm going to be a doctor just like Dad wants, and you totally suck at science and he doesn't even care. You could join Clown College if you wanted and he'd still treat you like a princess." I'm surprised that Nahal feels that way. I always assumed she was naturally perfect. I didn't realize she had to work really hard at it—or that she felt the same kind of pressure I do to please Mom and Dad.

"I think Dad would still love you, even if you didn't want to be a doctor," I tell her.

Nahal shrugs at the suggestion and grins. "I've come around to it. I'll probably go into plastic surgery. Lots of money in it."

I smile and give her a hug. She seems surprised at first and then hugs me back. When we let go, it feels like we're sisters again, just like when we were kids. I climb out of the car and look up at the hotel, excited to see Saskia.

When I get to Saskia's room, it's packed with kids I've never seen before, most of them not from our school. I recognize some college freshmen from the BU party, and Ashley and Robert are just leaving.

"Hey, drama queen," Ashley says as politely as possible. Robert is drinking from a Solo cup, and from the way he smells, I'd rather not think of what he's mixed together.

"You guys are leaving?" I ask, kind of surprised since Robert seems to have a place to drink.

"Yeah, I'm going to drive Sloppy McFeelyhands home and then break up with him." Robert leans his head against a wall and seems to be singing to himself. "I should always date older men." She was totally seeing Mr. Harris! "This party's so weird. I don't know anyone here, and there are some old-looking guys and I don't even want to know what they're doing in that room." I'm kind of freaked out but try not to show it.

"Have you seen Saskia anywhere?" I ask, looking around the room.

She looks at me like she has some delicious gossip to share. She whispers, "You're over Greg, right?"

I was never *under* Greg. "Of course I am. What does that have to do with anything?"

Robert is singing louder now and it almost sounds like screaming. Ashley walks over and has him sit on the floor so he doesn't hurt himself. She continues to whisper. "Greg, well, he, um . . ."

What is all this about Greg? What, he's crushing on someone else now? He played spin the bottle or something? I could care less.

"He and Saskia hooked up. Or they *are* hooking up."

I feel like I have been punched in the vagina. I don't hear the rest of what Ashley has to say. She must be loving this moment. I glance over at Saskia's bedroom door and see a DO NOT DISTURB sign on the doorknob.

"Yeah, I'm totally over Greg," I tell her, keeping a brave face. "You better go, Robert's waiting."

"Sucks to be you, bitch," she says as she pats me on the shoulder.

When she leaves I go to the bathroom and lock the door. I sit on the cold floor tiles and cry my little lesbian heart out. Nothing really makes sense. I didn't know Saskia even liked Greg! How could I have been so stupid! Of course she didn't like *me*. Why would she? She's so beautiful and I'm just cute.

The tears keep coming. Eventually there's a knock on the door.

"Hey, are you puking? 'Cause I've got to take a piss," says a male voice.

"Go away!" I yell but he keeps knocking. Too bad. He can pee on the carpet for all I care. I'm staying in here the rest of the night. I can hear him and others complain about the bathroom being locked, but after fifteen minutes the place seems to have quieted down a little. I wash my face in the sink and take deep breaths. I have to leave here sometime. I'm just not ready to. The next knock is Saskia.

"Whoever is in there, you are hogging the restroom!" she yells. I don't know if I want to see her right now. But maybe Ashley was just being cruel.

"It's Leila." She doesn't say anything for a moment.

"Leila, can you let me in? Please?"

Her voice is so much sweeter now. How can I even look at her? I'm so embarrassed and angry.

"Oh, come on, Leila, don't be mean. Let me in."

"Don't be mean? Are you kidding me?" I yell back.

"You open this door or I'll get one of these brutes to ram it down for me! Be a good girl, come on." I unlock the door and she enters, her hair mussed from something I'd rather not think about. She eyes me up and down. "I love your outfit! That color looks great on you!" I could throw up. "Are you angry at me?" she asks. Is she serious? "You told me you don't like Greg anymore! He's fair game, isn't he?"

"What about *us*?" I ask her with what I'm sure are disgusting wounded-bunny eyes.

"Us? What do you mean? We're friends."

"But, but we kissed! The other night ..."

"Girls do that all the time. Haven't you ever been to a sleepover before? Played truth or dare?" She's serious.

"But we weren't playing. I wasn't—" I stop talking and feel myself crying again.

"Come on, Leila. We had fun, but I'm not like that. I mean, really, what would we do together? I can't even look at my own vagina in the mirror, you know? It's just gross. No offense."

I sit down on the edge of the bathtub, with my face in my hands. I can't look at her. After a moment I feel her sit next to me.

"Look, you're a good friend. You're funny and talented. Didn't being in the show tonight prove that to you? Come on. Don't be upset with me. Is this the thanks I get for putting you in the show?"

I look up from my hands and wipe my tears away. "What do you mean, putting me in the show?"

Saskia smirks and rests her head on my shoulder. "Maybe a certain actress got sick from some baked goods I made her. You know, a good luck gift from her costar." I just stare at her in disbelief. She looks back, annoyed at my disapproval. "You wanted to be in the show, didn't you?"

"Yeah, but not like that! What did you give her?"

Saskia stands up and checks her makeup in the mirror. "Relax, she's not going to die or anything. I just added some ipecac and some samples my dad gets for work with brownie mix. She'll be back to her boring self in no time." Saskia fixes her hair a little bit and squints in a way that makes her look like a predatory cat. "Besides, the audience loved us together! You should be delighted! Kessler will definitely cast you in the next show."

I just stare at her with my mouth open.

"Look, Leila, you're being a bit of a downer. Let's get back out there. There's still plenty to drink and I sent Greg home. It's so difficult breaking in virgins. They get all starry-eyed after." She extends her hand to me but I refuse to take it.

"You're not a nice person, are you?" I say, angry. She pulls her hand away and looks at me, cocking an eyebrow.

"Nice girls are boring, Leila. Everybody knows that." We look at each other for a few seconds more before she opens the door. "Cheer up, won't you? No one likes a party pooper." And then she leaves. When I finally exit the bathroom, I have to bump my way through the crowd that practically rushes the open door. I don't cry again until I get to the elevator. I text Nahal to pick me up. Because this never happens, she knows I must be in trouble and says she'll be over as soon as possible.

TWENTY-ONE

I call Tess over the weekend but she never calls back. On Monday, in English class, I find out why. Ms. Taylor tells us that Tess is sick at home and spent a night in the hospital. She asks if someone can take Tess's homework to her, and I volunteer immediately. I feel guilty for something I didn't do. It's hard to focus for the rest of the class. Lisa leans over and writes on the edge of my notebook.

Do you want to talk about it?

Everyone's been buzzing all morning about Saskia and Greg hooking up. I've been avoiding Greg and Saskia all day and would like to avoid them for as long as possible. I don't want to talk to anybody. I look at Lisa and shake my head.

Science is even worse. Mr. Harris yells at me for not paying attention, and I mumble an apology, but really I can't wait to get out of his class. After school Mom drives me to see Tess. Her mom greets us and leads me to Tess's room while the two moms go off to get coffee. I don't really know what to say to Tess. She starts.

"How was the show?"

"Awful. I forgot all the lines and everyone laughed. That role was yours from the get-go."

She smiles and it makes me feel a little better. "You'll definitely be a shoo-in for the next show," I go on. "Kessler would be nuts not to cast you."

"Thanks. It was cool feeling like a star for a while," she says. "I know what people say about me. What they think about me. Honestly, it doesn't bother me so much. In a few years I'll be at Stanford or Emory, meet kids like me, finally be rid of my stupid retainer and maybe get a boyfriend. And Ashley and Robert, all those jerks? They'll do all right, but they'll still be unhappy. That's why they're so mean. I almost feel sorry for them."

"Don't. They don't deserve it," I say loudly. Tess shifts in her bed, looking out the window.

"It just would have been nice for them to see me

differently. Next show, I guess. Thanks for bringing me my work."

"I'm just glad you're feeling better."

"The doctor said I had an allergic reaction. I don't know what I'm allergic to, but they'll figure it out. " I should tell her the truth. But I think I'm just going to be a coward instead. We watch TV for the next half hour, as Maury Povich tells us who the real fathers of a bunch of illegitimate babies are. Eventually our moms come back from the kitchen and tell us to stop watching that junk.

The next few days at school I'm semicatatonic. I haven't slept because I'm worried about Saskia doing something nuts, I'm worried that Tomas and the tech girls know I'm gay, I'm worried about my parents finding out about me, I'm worried about the winter finals that are coming up, and I worry about Tess. I haven't been studying much. Ms. Taylor has noticed that I haven't been participating in class and says she's concerned about my other subjects. The dark circles around my eyes may have sort of tipped her to something, too. I tell her I don't really care about much.

"Is something wrong at home?" she asks.

"No."

"Are you being bullied?"

"No."

"Are you going to tell me what's wrong?"

"No."

"Is this getting us anywhere?"

"No."

"Did someone break your heart?" She sure is perceptive. I bite my lip and look at the ground. She takes a deep breath. This should be interesting.

She grins in a kind of manic fashion. "Leila, I know what it is to be brokenhearted. A great many people in the world do. It is one of the worst pains a person can know. And so I empathize. However, I've learned that moping doesn't get you anywhere."

"I guess not, no."

"And we're awesome, right? I mean we're real catches . . . we're wonderful! And we'd better stop this moping," she says, getting worked up like she's a football coach trying to hype us up for a game. "We're both going to pick ourselves up and we're going to live again, because they're the assholes, not us." This is not exactly her most eloquent speech, but she's right.

"Thanks, Ms. Taylor."

When we exit the classroom, Mr. Harris is making a bunch of the popular girls in the hallway laugh and Saskia is sitting on Greg's lap in a vestibule. Ms. Taylor and I just look at each other, miserably.

"I'm going to the cafeteria," Ms. Taylor says before she hoofs it down the hall. I can't be in the same area as Saskia. I walk out to the parking lot to have a good cry by the tennis courts. I'm pathetic. I'm stupid. I'm depressed.

"Want a Raisinet?"

I'm not alone.

I look up to see Lisa Katz at the base of the bleachers, wearing a long winter coat and smoking. She's so cavalier about doing it on school grounds. I wipe my tears away and chuckle. She sits next to me and we don't talk about when I last saw her. We just sit together, sharing Raisinets, and watch the middle school tennis players in their winter coats missing volleys in the distance.

TWENTY-TWO

The distractions of the holidays keep me pretty busy at the beginning of winter break. Though my family doesn't technically do Christmas, we exchange gifts around a plastic tree.

But after Christmas my mother notices that I am gloomier than ever. I hate that I'm so full of angst; it's such a cliché. Saskia wouldn't be doing cliché things. *Stop thinking about her!* I have to remind myself to stop thinking about her because she's an awful person who hurt Tess. But for some reason I keep dreaming about her. I've had a recurring dream in which I am in an enchanted forest, like something out of a Disney movie. Saskia is singing like Aurora from *Sleeping Beauty*, and all kinds of woodland creatures crowd around her. She looks so gorgeous, I want to be near her, too. I get closer, and a bird perches on her finger as she sings a high note. Then her eyes go wide and she bites the bird's head off. I usually wake up after that.

Anyway, Mom has noticed my mood and Dad has noticed my science grade. Neither of them is all that pleased with me right now, but they can't really ground me since I've just been in my room by myself anyway. I'm pretty sure I overheard Dad ask Nahal if I was on drugs. Mom finally forces me to invite some people to the house for pizza.

So I invite Tess, Tomas, and the tech girls to come over. The day of the party, if you can call it that, Mom is setting up the living room table with cookies, a veggie platter, and soda to go with the pizzas. She thought everyone might like hot tea, but I told her they wouldn't miss it. She tells me she'll be upstairs with Dad and will pretend like they aren't even at home, but if anyone needs a Band-Aid, Advil, tampon, cold compress, life vest, or tourniquet, I should come get her.

Eventually everyone arrives and we all just sit around the table, staring at one another. Tomas sits glumly, his arms crossed over his chest. Taryn slouches. Simone nibbles at a mushroom slice. Christina is wearing the pair of fangs I bought her for running the booth so well the night I had to perform in the play, and she tongues the tip of her elongated canine again and again. Tess, who has been almost as depressed as I have by the Greg-Saskia hookup, looks out of the corner of her eye at Christina's fangs. I can't tell whether she's freaked out or studying how they mold to Christina's teeth.

"Great party," Taryn says, flicking a carrot at Tomas's head.

"It was nice of you to have us over, Leila," Tess says.

"Yes. It reminds me of a fourth-grade birthday party," says Tomas. Tess lays her head on the table, and Simone plays party cheerleader.

"The hummus is fabulous! Did your mom make it?" Simone asks.

"No, it's store-bought," I say.

"It's a traditional Middle Eastern food, so I just wondered."

"Yeah, it's traditional in most Arab countries, but Persians are not Arab, so . . ." Saskia would have known that. She can share all her cultural knowledge with Greg now.

"Oh. Right." The silence after is unbearable, until the doorbell rings. I don't know who would be selling Jehovah at this time of night. I overhear my mom open the door, then thank whoever is there for coming. When the mystery guest arrives in the kitchen, Tomas shifts upward happily in his seat at the prospect of fresh entertainment; Taryn defensively crosses her arms; and Tess remains head down on the table. Mom enters the kitchen with her arm around Lisa.

"Look who I invited? Wasn't it nice of her to come?" I feel the color rise in my cheeks at the thought of Lisa taking in this sorry scene. As Mom deposits Lisa and obliviously walks away, the others gape. Lisa's a cool kid. What is she doing here?

"So you wanted to see how the other half lives or something?" Taryn asks. Simone nudges her to cut it out. Tomas puts his hand under his chin like an interviewer and smiles.

"I love your ponytail!" Tomas is in full kiss-ass mode. Ponytail? Really? Lisa turns her attention to me.

"Your mom called my mom to wish her a happy Hanukkah and they got to talking about how antisocial their daughters are. And here I am. Happy Kwanzaa."

"You guys celebrate Kwanzaa?" Simone asks, not really catching on.

"Well, it's nice to have someone stylish here," Tomas interjects. "I'm surprised Saskia isn't here." I crumple like a tissue at the mention of her name.

"Tomas, she's dating Greg! Leila's kind of ex! Why would she be invited?" Tess asks. At least the comment got her head off the table.

"Greg's a catch, but I feel like she's too much woman for him," Tomas says.

"I don't like that girl at all. There's something about her I don't trust," Taryn says, flicking yet another carrot at Tomas's head. He gives her a look like he's ready to smear hummus on her face.

"Yeah, she seems like a phony to me," Lisa says, and my head jerks upward. She seems to deliberately be avoiding eye contact with me.

"How very Holden Caulfield of you," says Tomas. "I *was* upset she didn't invite me to the drama party."

"You didn't miss anything." I say to shut this conversation down. Silence descends again, until Tomas suggests we play truth or dare. None of us takes the bait, but he continues anyway.

"Okay, Tess, truth or dare?"

"Must we reduce ourselves to this?"

"I'll make it tame, I promise," Tomas says as he crosses his heart and hopes to die. Tess eyes him with suspicion but nods. She picks truth.

"Okay, if you only had twenty-four hours to live, what would you do?" Tess thinks about it. After what seems like forever, she begins to speak.

"I guess first I'd get up and brush my teeth—" We all groan, and Tomas cuts her off.

"Forget it, Tess. I'll start with someone else." He surveys the circle and lands on Lisa.

"Lisa, truth or dare?"

Lisa rolls her eyes but plays along. "Truth."

"Who was your first crush?" Lisa suddenly gets quiet and I think she might even be blushing. Tomas is intrigued. "Well? Go on. It's a very tame question."

Lisa smiles at him. "I change to dare then. The truth is just too embarrassing."

Tomas is getting annoyed. "This is the worst game of truth or dare ever!" he pronounces to the rabble.

"I have a dare for you," Taryn says, glaring at Lisa. "Monday lunch period, you sit with Tess in the cafeteria." Tess's face turns mauve and Tomas gasps. Lisa, being one of the cool kids, would never even consider sitting with someone like Tess.

"You can't do it, can you?" Taryn fumes. "Ruin your stupid high-school status? Sure, Tess is mousy and probably still speaks to her Bratz dolls, but at least she has a brain and she uses it. You just go about with your flock, doing what's expected of you." Simone holds Taryn's arm, trying to calm her down.

"I don't have Bratz dolls," Tess whispers, swirling a carrot in the hummus.

"Whatever. Do you or do you not have a poster of Neil deGrasse Tyson above your bed?" Taryn asks. Tess blushes and Taryn continues with her spiel. "You think I don't hear what your friends call me under their breath?"

"You're right," Lisa says confidently, staring Taryn right in the eye.

"What?" Taryn asks.

"My friends do treat people badly sometimes. Frankly, I haven't really felt like hanging out with anybody lately, cool group or not. None of it really matters. I only ever cared what one person thought of me, but he's gone now. So sure, Tess, I'd love to sit with you at lunch. If I don't ditch. But that's not going to make the world a better place."

Lisa raises an eyebrow at Taryn. "And *you* need to stop pretending that high school social groups don't affect you. After all, you've created one for yourself." Lisa motions to Simone and Christina.

"That's true," Tomas says. "And you say awful things to people all the time."

"This is a stupid party!" Taryn says. And my mom thought this would be fun.

Lisa picks up a baby carrot and points it in my direction. "Truth or dare?" I know Lisa saw Saskia and me kiss in the bathroom. I don't like feeling that she has something she can lord over me, but she would have said something to Ashley or Robert already if she was interested in spreading gossip. Everyone here except Tess knows about my feelings for Saskia anyway, so it's not them I'm worried about. Would Lisa dare say anything with my parents upstairs?

I'm not ready for the truth. "Dare," I say without flinching. Tomas edges to the front of his seat, awaiting something juicy. Lisa's silence charges the room. The smallest movement could bring on a shock.

"Show them your scruff day photos," Lisa says before picking up a wide slice of cheeseless pizza.

"What on earth is scruff day?" Tomas asks, and Lisa pulls a long strand of cheese from her slice with mirth in her eyes. I shake my head and giggle a little for the first time all evening.

"I have no idea where they are," I protest.

Lisa isn't giving up. "We can always ask your mom. I can go get her," Lisa says as she drops her pizza and stands up. She begins to run out of the living room toward the stairs.

I race after her and tug the back of her shirt. She stumbles backward, laughing and swatting at my arm.

"Mrs. Azadi!" she yells, and the bedroom door opens. I put my hand over Lisa's mouth, but she licks my palm and I pull it away and wipe it on my jeans. Gross.

"Yes, girls?" Mom asks from upstairs.

Minutes later Mom has started a home movie of Lisa and me on the TV, and Taryn is laughing harder than any of the rest of us at footage of a Halloween parade at our elementary school.

"Oh, you guys were so cute!" Mom says, having sat herself right between Lisa and me on the couch. I'd be embarrassed by all this if I weren't so depressed. We are in second grade, and Lisa is dressed as Cinderella and I am dressed as a pumpkin.

"Did you guys mean to do that?" Simone asks, pointing at our younger selves on TV. I say no and Lisa says yes at the same time. I lean over Mom to look at Lisa, who keeps her attention on the television.

"Leila kept bragging about how her mom got her a pumpkin costume," Lisa says.

"Such a cute outfit!" Mom says, pinching my cheek, and Taryn laughs some more. This is mortifying.

"She kept talking about how excited she was, so I

wanted to join in," Lisa lies. I had complained how much Mom loved the pumpkin costume, and I hated it but didn't want to hurt her feelings. Lisa showed up in a Cinderella costume and made me feel better. She said that way we could go to the ball together.

"Halloween is the best thing ever," Christina says as she studies the pageantry, trying to figure out all the costumes.

"Christina likes Halloween all year round," Taryn says. Christina bears her fangs and hisses at her. Mom grabs my hand tightly as though Christina might actually strike.

"Why don't I cut you guys some watermelon?" Mom asks, only it sounds like "*vatermelon*" and makes me think of Lisa's Mom's long-ago comments. Mom gets up and makes sure not to step on Tomas, who is lounging on the rug.

"I actually love Halloween, too," says Simone. "It's nondenominational, kids get candy, grown-ups party, everybody wins."

"I've never been crazy about the pranks," says Tomas.

"Yeah, but I love that you get to be whatever you want on Halloween," Tess says. "It's like living with a fantasy identity for one day." Tess then looks at Christina. "Is that why you do it?" Christina cocks her head to the side and ponders the question.

"I hate to break this to you, but vampires are passé," Tomas says. "What with *Twilight* and *True*—" He's interrupted by a feral growl from Christina.

"Do *not* say the T-word in my presence. Ever." Christina says it with conviction and anger. Guess she's not a Twihard. "I pay homage to the old ones because I like the idea of being forever young. When you were a kid, don't you remember just having *full* days when you were absolutely elated? Like when you can't wait for your birthday because you're so excited or you read a book you love and want to share it with everyone. Adults lose that. They have moments of happiness, maybe. Don't you see how they are? They judge, they get angry, they worry; they want things before time runs out but never go after them. I don't want to be like that."

This is the most I've ever heard Christina speak. I think this is the most Taryn or Simone has heard her speak, too, because they are paying her their full attention. The home movie of Lisa and me sitting by each other at a Halloween party continues. Eight-year-old Lisa is laughing while eight-year-old me sticks my tongue out at her.

"Why not dress like Peter Pan then?" Tomas asks, not really understanding Christina's behavior.

"Can you see me in green tights?" Christina is wearing black jeans, a *Nosferatu* T-shirt Taryn made for her, and purple streaks in her hair. We collectively shake our heads. "Besides, I'm dressed like a lost boy." We look at her in confusion. "Eighties vampire flick. *The Lost Boys.*" No one knows what she's talking about. "We're going to need to have a vampire movie marathon. Minus the T-word."

Mom walks in with a giant bowl filled with chunks of watermelon. "Oh, I wish you all came over all the time. It's so nice having the house full." She gazes at the TV. "Look how happy you were," she says with a hint of sadness. She puts the bowl of watermelon on the center table. "I was never here! Good night, everyone!"

I feel Lisa look at me. "Dare is over. Your turn."

"I dare everyone to watch *Zombie Killers Part II* right now."

By the end of the night, after all the screaming and laughter only an epic like *Zombie Killers Part II* could produce, the group starts to break up. Tess is the first to wave good night to everyone and then head upstairs. I insisted she sleep over because I feel protective of her after her trip to the hospital.

"Vampire movie marathon. We're setting it up on the screens in the auditorium." It's a command, not a suggestion, from Christina, and I nod because it's incredible to see her enthusiastic about something.

Simone gives me a big hug. "Tell your beautiful mom she is an excellent hostess."

Taryn just lightly punches me on the shoulder. Then the tech crew girls grab their coats and drift outside to pile into Taryn's car.

"Well, you sure know how to throw a soiree." Tomas says, oozing with sarcasm.

I ooze it right back. "Glad you could fit it into your busy schedule." He pinches my cheek just like my mom did, and he winks before exiting. Lisa's the only one left. It's strange to think that the night would not have gone so well without her. Okay, it was headed for complete disaster.

"Thanks for coming," I say. "I'm sure there was other stuff you could have done."

"You can thank your mom for that. I always liked her more than you," she replies, straight-faced. Then she kicks my foot with hers to let me know she's joking. We stand in silence for a moment. "It was you, you know."

"What was me?"

"My first crush." Before I have a chance to process what she's said, I'm gazing at her back as she glides smoothly into her soft leather jacket and strides swiftly to her much too fancy car.

TWENTY-THREE

The rest of break I kept replaying in my mind what Lisa said. And I still can't make sense of it. Mostly I just don't believe it's possible. And she's spent so much time avoiding me at Armstead.

And then break is over. Going back wouldn't be so bad if Saskia weren't around. From the first day she soaks up all the male attention in the cafeteria. I'm sure it pisses Ashley off, because all the boys who used to sit at her table move to sit with Saskia, every one of them trying to impress her in some way or another. There is a new queen of the castle, and everyone knows it.

From my usual table, I watch Robert try to get Saskia's attention, pantomiming some story about snowboarding, or at least it looks like snowboarding. Greg sits next to Saskia, who has linked her arm through his. It's sort of funny trying to watch him eat using one hand while Saskia plays with the other. Greg catches my eye, and I quickly turn my head away. I'm still angry with him, but he doesn't know it or have any idea why.

Lisa and I haven't talked since my raging party. I still don't know what to make of her confession. Did it mean she's gay? Did it mean that she *still* likes me? Did she just say it to make me feel better about the whole Saskia situation? I never even considered Lisa as an option. That doesn't mean I should now. I can't begin to entertain any thoughts other than what the hell I'm going to do about science this semester and avoiding Saskia.

Tess places her lunch tray across from me, sits down, and removes her retainer. I'm thankful someone is blocking the view. "I watched all of the *Zombie Killers* films over break. They were great!" Tess exclaims. "I had to suspend disbelief about the science behind it, but the main character was surprisingly full of pathos. You know, before he disemboweled his best friend with a rusty spoon." She takes a bite of her grilled cheese sandwich. I appreciate that Tess is still willing to eat grilled cheese along with me. We're the only ones left in our grade; all the other girls just eat salad.

Saskia laughs loudly, and I can't resist looking past Tess to see what's so funny. Greg is sort of wincing and Robert has a grin on his face, the kind that can't mean anything good.

I hear a familiar voice before I sense a new arrival at our table. "May I sit with you?" I look up to see Lisa standing beside Tess's chair. She's changed her hair, brushed her bangs out of her eyes. Tess gapes up at Lisa, who quietly waits for her to respond. Of course: the dare.

"If you don't mind our discussion of *Zombie Killers*," Tess says at last, and Lisa sits down next to her. The cafeteria becomes much quieter. Ashley cranes to look at Lisa from her table, her nose scrunched and forehead wrinkled in confusion. It's not a good look for her. Lisa pretends everyone isn't staring.

"You don't have to go through with the dare," I mumble, slumping in my seat.

Lisa takes a sip of her tea from a paper cup, calmly and without batting an eye. "What dare?" She knows what dare. She's just acting like this is normal behavior. I'm really sick of everyone acting like things are normal when they aren't. You can't just say something like "You were my first crush" like it's perfectly natural, and not explain yourself!

"So, *Zombie Killers*. I've only seen the first two," Lisa says. "Any point in seeing the others?"

"I actually thought the fourth installment had promise, but that subplot with the radioactive rodents was over the top. But in the third—"

"What is this? What's happening here?" I demand. Tess and Lisa stare at me. "Greg and I talk about *Zombie Killers*. Greg. And he's over at the asshat table. *You*,"—I address Lisa, staring her right in the eye—"decide to be friends again after *years* of pretending like I don't exist. And then you tell me . . ." I almost forget where I am and that Tess is sitting with us. "Tell me something out of the blue and act like everything is just fine! Well, everything is not fine!" I must have said that a little louder than I thought I did because people are staring at *me* now.

Lisa blinks a few times. Ugh, she's so exasperating! She turns to Tess. "So the fourth one isn't so great, huh?" Tess just shakes her head and looks perplexed. I groan.

Lisa turns back to me. "I'm sorry I wasn't brave enough to be your *friend* back then. But I'd like to be honest with you again. When you're ready. And when we aren't surrounded by so many spectators." I deflate and droop in my seat. She's right. It's not the place to have this conversation.

"The *Zombie Killers Part V* trailer is amazing," I mutter.

I look over at Greg because he would know what I'm talking about, but he's hanging on to Saskia's every word, just like all the other guys at their table. She's probably telling them the best ways to poison someone.

"Hi-ho, losers." Taryn saunters up to our table, Christina and Simone in tow. Taryn quirks an eyebrow when she sees Lisa sitting with us. "Well, I'll give you credit. You do honor your dares."

"Nice to see you, too, Taryn," Lisa says.

"You guys working on the play this term?" I ask.

"Yes. *The Importance of Being Earnest* doesn't really inspire me, but I'm looking forward to finding period costumes," Simone says. "Do you think you'll work on the play with us?" I can't imagine having to watch people in petticoats over and over again.

"I'd like to do theater again, but I want to try something other than stage-managing," I say.

"I'm designing the set for the middle school play. We need student directors if you're interested," Christina says. Direct? Me? Molding the future actors of tomorrow? Kids adore me!

"Yeah! I'd love that," I blurt before I have time to overthink it.

"Cool. I'll let Kessler know you're interested. Tomas

wouldn't be able to handle them all by himself," Christina says. Tomas! He's going to take over everything!

The tech girls wave and walk out of the cafeteria. "Well, no sports again for me," I say cheerily. Lisa just shakes her head and Tess laughs.

"So now I can run for real during squash practice?" Tess asks with a smirk.

"I will not stand in the way of your varsity dreams now that you're buddies with the all-star here," I say with a nod to Lisa.

Lisa finishes, chewing an orange slice before she answers. "I don't know that I'm going to play this year." Tess gasps a little because she knows how good Lisa is. She's better at squash than she is at soccer, if that's possible.

I feel myself getting angry. "You loved it, though. Plus, you're really good. You're good at basically everything." Lisa sets her jaw and looks at me. I match her gaze and see her eyes have gone dull with refusal. Not even a glimmer of a shine.

"Why, Leila, I didn't know you cared," Lisa says. Tess just looks back and forth between us like a fight is about to start.

"If you don't try out, I'll have my mom tell your mom,"

I say in the most threatening tone I can muster. It must not be very effective; Lisa just chuckles.

"Oh no. Not that. How will I survive?"

"If you don't try out, I'll . . . I'll . . ." I can't think of anything to hold over her. She holds up her hands to stop me.

"I will try out if you agree to hang out once in a while." She's serious. She wants to be friends again. Or something more? The *something* freaks me out . . . but maybe in a good way.

"Okay," I whisper. Lisa and I study each other for a moment. Like we are the cowboys sizing each other up in *Zombie Killers Part III*, just about to detonate the water tower and drown the town. A little bit of a spark has returned to her eyes, which are really pretty with those bangs off her face.

"You guys are weird," Tess says, and takes a bite of her grilled cheese sandwich. Tess really has no gaydar. But apparently neither do I.

"What's up with you? Why are you avoiding me again?" Greg asks when he corners me by my locker at the end of the day. I keep my attention on the locker's contents for as long as possible, stalling for a way to explain myself.

There's a picture on the door of Greg and me posing like we're hard thugs, both of us wearing black Dickies skullcaps, standing back-to-back. I can't believe a girl is coming between us.

"You're going to be late for wrestling tryouts," I say, and he touches my shoulder so I'll face him. I fold my arms and refuse to meet his glance.

"You didn't call or text all break. Didn't even wish me a happy New Year. That's messed up." I stare at my shoes. What can I say to him? I'm angry with him but it's not his fault. I'm angry with him and I can't begin to tell him why.

"Yeah, well, you've made some new friends lately," I mutter in a voice barely audible to the human ear. "I didn't want to get in the way."

He's heard me just fine. "Is that what this is about? My seeing Saskia?" He chuckles, but it's mean sounding. "Why do you care who I date, Leila?"

I stare him right in his stupid eyes. "I *don't* care who you date!" It isn't true, though. I care that he's dating *her*. I'm glad people are off to their afternoon activities and not in the hallway to watch Greg and me argue.

Greg grunts in frustration. "I don't get you! You told me you weren't interested in dating me. So I can't date anyone else?" He's so dense, always making this about him.

This isn't fair. I want to tell my friend what's wrong, what's happening.

"I just don't think she's right for you," I say, and I really mean that. He doesn't know what she's capable of or that she broke my heart in giant, jagged pieces. Greg is trying to read me, but I won't let him. I'm working hard to keep any emotion off my face.

"Hi, guys!" Saskia calls, bounding down the hall to us. So much for not showing emotion. I wince a little as she gives Greg a peck on the lips. She puts her arm around his waist like he's going to run away if she doesn't hold him as tightly as possible. "Hi, sweetie!" she says to me. Is she seriously calling me *sweetie*? I want to scream but can't let Greg know something is wrong.

"Hey." That's all she's getting out of me.

"Did you have a nice break?" she asks with a saccharine smile. Like nothing has happened. Like she didn't inspect my mouth with her tongue whenever it was convenient.

"Yeah. Pretty quiet," I say trying not to get intoxicated by her scent again. She smells like expensive perfume and waxy lipstick. "You were busy, I bet."

Greg just rolls his eyes and stares off to the side. "I better get to wrestling. I'll see you later?" he asks Saskia. She kisses his cheek before he saunters off, not even looking in my direction. I watch him stride down the hallway and out the door. I want to yell at him but I can't. I hate this.

"He has such a nice bum," Saskia says. "But he's so *boring*. What did you two even talk about?" I twist to glare at her. She seems to genuinely be waiting for my answer.

"There's something wrong with you," I say, slamming my locker shut. She doesn't even blink.

"I'm just trying to be polite," she says. "Look, I know you're probably not over me, but I thought we could at least be friends. You're the only person that makes me laugh in this place." I'm tired of being her source of entertainment. I walk away, but she follows me. "If you're upset about my being with Greg, I can break up with him." I stop walking. The hall, the whole school is spinning around me. I'm dizzy with rage.

"Why would you do that to him?" I ask through clenched teeth. I don't want Greg to be hurt just because I have been. Saskia grabs my hand and turns me around to face her.

"Because we're friends, aren't we? Isn't that what friends do for each other?" No. That's not what friends do for each other. I'm wondering exactly how many *friends* Saskia has had in her lifetime. She grasps my hand a little tighter now.

"Don't you like him?" I ask, incredulous.

Saskia just bites her lower lip. "He has his merits." She says it like she's talking about a restaurant. "But I'd rather hang out with you." She inches a little closer and as much as I'm upset with her . . . Wow, have her eyes always been that green?

I blink to break the spell, and try to make her understand. "Greg's my friend, so I want him to be happy, and I don't want to see him hurt. You should date someone you really like. But you can't just play with people. " Saskia gives me a blank look. "You know, toy with their emotions and toss them when you're bored?" It still doesn't register. I try again. "Poison their brownies?"

Saskia pulls me in a little closer. My hand brushes her breast and I blush. "I promise. I'll be more conscientious of others." I want to believe her. I really do. People make mistakes, right? Even gorgeous girls who are really good at kissing, but bad—BAD—for hurting people. She pulls me in by my arm and embraces me, nestling her head in the crook of my neck. I hate that part of me is creeped out and part of me is tingly. Emotions are so stupid. Zombies have it easy.

TWENTY-FOUR

Mr. Kessler has given Tomas and me the reins to choose and direct the middle school play since he's going to be so busy with *The Importance of Being Earnest*. Tomas suggested doing *Glengarry Glen Ross*. Mr. Kessler went pale and suggested we think along the lines of a one-act fairy tale. I suggest "Cinderella," thinking of Lisa.

"'Cinderella'? That's so tired," says Libby, a seventh grader with a lisp. The six other kids who signed up for the play, five girls and one boy, chime their agreement.

"Let's do a play version of *Goodfellas*!" That Thurston Smith kid sure has a lot of energy. He gets the rest of the cast to cheer and Tomas tries to settle them down. I don't know that we are cut out for this. Tomas blows a whistle and they finally shut up. I think my eardrum is busted.

"*Goodfellas* is an incredibly violent movie," Tomas says. "And rated R, which leads me to question your parents' child-rearing skills." I look at the cast in front of us. The kids are awkward and fidgety, and they listen to Tomas like he's the coolest person on the planet. Oh, what a few years will do.

"My older brother showed it to me, and it was *awesome*!" Thurston exclaims, pretending to fire a machine gun.

"What if we rewrite 'Cinderella'? Make it . . . less tired?" I'm surprised by my initiative. Apparently so is Tomas.

"Why, Leila! You're actually onto something," he says, clapping his hands together. "And I thought I was going to have to carry the load of this production myself. What do you think, guys?"

"Can we have gangsters in it? Like Cinderella has a glass gun instead of slipper?" Thurston asks. The rest of the cast cheers his suggestion. Tomas blows the whistle again. I have a feeling I know how the rest of the play rehearsals are going to go.

After some improvisation games, like the human knot

and freeze, which help us get to know the kids and figure out a little more about them, Tomas and I end rehearsal early so we can brainstorm our new version of "Cinderella."

We walk from the middle school down the hill to the upper school. "What if Cinderella is in a corporate setting, and instead of being concerned with her glass slipper, she's concerned with the glass ceiling?" I suggest. Tomas looks at me like I am the biggest dork in the universe.

"Leila, they're kids. But I like the different, contemporary setting. What if we make Cinderella gender nonconforming?" Tomas asks.

"I'm not so sure about that." I don't know how that would go over in middle school. And I don't want to be associated with more out-of-the-box stuff than I have to be right now. Tomas gives me side eye that would make a person of weaker character cry.

"The administration is always going on about how they *love* and support diversity, so they'd be hypocrites to disapprove," he says. "We'll write a tasteful story that gets people to think about their hateful, ignorant, stupid reactions to things they do not understand."

"I just think we might be over our heads already, and to make a fairy tale controversial, well ..."

"Leila! We have a chance to tell a story that can get people thinking. Aren't you sick of being a wallflower? I know you are, because you're not stage-managing again."

"Okay. We'll write the play. So long as we don't call it *Cinderfella*. That would just scream amateur."

TWENTY-FIVE

Ms. Taylor is making us read aloud from the essays she assigned before break. To get any of us to read aloud is like pulling teeth. Usually I help her out and volunteer because I feel bad, but this time someone beats me to the punch. Ms. Taylor is shocked when Lisa raises her hand.

"Is it okay if it's creative nonfiction?" Lisa asks.

"Oh! Lisa! That would be wonderful. Please, go right ahead," Ms. Taylor says. Lisa pulls out some tattered pages and walks to the front of the classroom. Ashley looks confused. Robert stops sipping from his Gatorade bottle. Tess, sitting beside me, whispers, "I didn't think she even did schoolwork anymore."

Lisa stands in the front of the class, staring down at

her pages. Her hand trembles only slightly. She takes a deep breath and begins to read.

"My therapist has told me to be more honest with my feelings, which I think is a crock of shit—" Ms. Taylor opens her mouth to say something but reconsiders and apparently decides to let the swear slide, maybe because Lisa is actually participating— "because no one is ever *really* honest. We talk to one another but never really say anything. We hide from things that are uncomfortable, things like death." I can't believe this is happening right now. The whole classroom is so silent you can hear everyone breathe.

"So he's dead now. Has been dead for a while and I get it. I understand that he's buried in the ground, I understand that grieving is a process, I understand that my mother is emotionally starved for his attention and no longer has it, so she's forcing me into her life. I understand all of that." Lisa takes another deep breath and blinks for a few moments. It feels like hours. "What I don't understand is that I should be over it by now. No one's ever *over* it, but I should concentrate on wanting to feel better. Distract myself. Get back into sports. Go shopping with the girls. And the only thing I've been distracting myself with are thoughts of you."

Ashley looks at the clock and sighs. Robert looks like he's tearing up a little as he takes a long sip from his bottle.

"I think of you and how I spent so much time trying *not* to think of you. How I pushed away traces of you, memories we shared as kids, all the things I never knew I cherished because I was scared. Scared of what being around you meant and what you could take away. What you have taken away." I have a feeling she's not talking about her brother, Steve, anymore.

"And if I'm supposed to be honest, if I'm supposed to feel things even when they are uncomfortable, I'd like to do that with you. I'm ready to be honest, because his dying taught me I don't want to waste any more time." Lisa pauses for a minute and her bottom lip quivers a little. She exhales and composes herself. "If you're ready to be honest, so am I." Holy crap, it is about me! I stare at the floor to avoid making eye contact with anyone—including Lisa. What she just did was bold and fearless. But she could have warned me. She may be ready, but I don't know if I am. I don't know if I can be that brave.

No one is breathing now. Only the sound of Lisa folding her paper, finished, breaks the silence.

"Thank you, Lisa, that was—" Before Ms. Taylor can even try to say *what* that was, Lisa has walked right out of the classroom, leaving her backpack behind.

I skip history class to go find her. Lisa is sitting at the

top of the bleachers, coatless, but seemingly unaffected by the cold and snow. I'm shivering, but not because of the temperature. I climb up the bleachers and stop a few risers in front of her. She looks out at the empty tennis courts, refusing to meet my eye.

"I don't understand you," I say. Lisa doesn't say anything so I go on, awkwardly. I have had a few make-out sessions, but it dawns on me that I've never had a conversation like this one. "Just to confirm, I am not reading anything into that public reading that you didn't intend—"

"It was about you," Lisa says and now fixes her eyes to mine. It makes me blush, but I can't look away.

"Lisa, are you . . . I mean, what are you?" She just smiles. How can someone be so unflinchingly blunt and remain so elusive? She's not gay. She couldn't be. It would be too easy to fall for her if she were. I don't think I could handle that.

"I'm sad mostly," Lisa says. "I didn't like certain feelings I had for you in sixth grade. It was just . . . weird. You were one of my best friends. When I came to Armstead, I figured that would be the end of it. Of my feelings for you, and of feeling *that way*."

My mind is *blown*. "Sixth grade! Seriously?" Lisa

chuckles a little at my surprise. She pats the seat beside her. I'm hesitant to climb up, but her gaze doesn't waver, and I make my way up the risers, as if I'm hypnotized. I sit next to her but far enough away that we can't touch. This feels too real, and it freaks me out a little. Lisa takes a cigarette from her pants pocket. She fumbles with a matchbook, her hands shaking so that she can't even strike a match. I take the matchbook from her hands.

"I don't condone this habit, just so you know," I say while striking a match for her. She leans closer to light her cigarette. She pulls away and takes a long drag.

"Anyway, I liked some boys okay enough and figured those feelings for you were a fluke." She slowly exhales a long wisp of smoke, sighing softly at the same time. "Then you showed up at my school. And it turned out I still liked you, which was really, really annoying. So I avoided you. Which wasn't so hard given the sandals with socks thing."

"That was just a couple of times!" I protest, and she chuckles again. She takes another long drag, as though it's what powers the exhalation of truth that follows.

She rolls her eyes. "I was doing fine until you were so ridiculously sweet at just the right times. You're crazy good at that by the way." My cheeks burn in the bitter cold. "But

I figured you were straight." Have I landed in some parallel universe where everyone is gay and I don't know it? If Ms. Taylor comes out next, I will die. "Then I saw you with *her* in the bathroom."

"Oh," I whisper. "She's seeing Greg now."

Lisa smirks and flicks her cigarette away. "I just want you to know that all of this is my therapist's fault, that bitch." I can't help laughing. "And that you have someone to talk to. If you want." I hear a twinge of hope in her voice.

"Thank you," I murmur. I wish I knew the right words to say. I don't know what this means for us, but I know it's really nice to have someone I can trust fully for the very first time.

"Does your mom know?" I ask. Lisa shakes her head.

"I figured there's no reason to tell her. I'm not dating anyone, so . . ." Lisa blushes, and wow. She's really serious about her feelings for me. "I assume you haven't told your parents?"

"Lisa, you don't understand. It would hurt them. I've already disappointed them. My father is desperate for me to be a doctor. They'd probably kick me out. You know where they're from, being gay is illegal? They imprison people over there for feeling like I do! Sentence them to death sometimes." My lip trembles and my eyes water, but I don't care if Lisa sees. She's seen everything else.

And then, there she is. The Lisa I knew so well. She takes my hand and rubs my wrist with her thumb. "Then it's a good thing you live in the good ole U-S-of-A. Let's get out of here. It's freezing."

TWENTY-SIX

Tess and I are sitting in the library, supposedly study-ing for a science test. But Tess never really has to study for anything, and she's going on and on about the Valentine's Dance, still weeks away. We won't have a prom in the spring because last year's seniors filled the swimming pools with bubble bath, so the Valentine's Dance, for all intents and purposes, is going to be our big formal occasion. All the girls in my grade are making a big deal about it.

"We should go shopping soon, before all the good dresses are taken," she says.

"I'll go shopping with you if you want, but I'm prob-ably not going to the dance," I tell her.

She's already jumped ahead. "We should get a group

together and rent a limo." I can't be too annoyed, because she really is a good friend to me. She could go with the girls from the squash team, who would be just as excited about it as she is, and leave me out, but she wants include me even though I'm being such a downer about it.

"What about dates?" I say, as though the answer to that question is not obvious.

"I could help," Saskia murmurs, creeping up behind us.

"No," I say, protective of Tess, even though Saskia is oblivious to Tess's feelings about Greg, and Tess seems to be moving on. Maybe she figured she had a chance when I was the obstacle to her happiness, but waiting for Greg to get over Saskia is a statistical impossibility.

"I could help you pick out dresses! Oh, come on, you know you're helpless, Leila. You have no fashion sense." Saskia winks, looking me up and down as though part of her is assessing my body in a slightly inappropriate way. I cross my arms over my chest. "Think of it as my charitable contribution. We can all go shopping. What do you say?"

I want to be on better terms with Saskia for Greg's sake. He and I haven't spoken since our argument. I also should be on better terms with Saskia because she knows I'm into girls, but I'd rather send her to Saint Petersburg on

Aeroflot. At least she's trying to be friendly, in her slightly warped Saskia way. And her hair looks so good down.

"It'll be great. You can get dresses for the dance, and we'll also find something for you both that will guarantee you'll get dates in the meantime." Saskia smiles at Tess like she's running for office, and Tess looks so hopeful I can almost ignore the feeling in my bones that this is a very bad idea.

Tess is doing her best to speak girl with Saskia, talking about upcoming spring collections, but it sounds rehearsed, like she's memorized information out of a magazine. She half gives up and walks beside me as we enter the next store. It feels like we have been to about thirty already. I can't quite figure out why Saskia has offered to do this, but if it helps Tess, that's all that matters. Maybe she's really making amends. I just don't know why I let myself be roped into it. I have no intention of going to the dance.

Saskia holds up hangers to Tess with the fervor of a *Project Runway* contestant. When Tess emerges from the changing room, she looks really good in the clothes Saskia has picked for her. I will give Saskia one thing; she does know fashion.

"Leila, you should totally try this on," Tess says, pulling

a red dress from the rack. Saskia looks at the dress and gushes about it, too.

"Excellent eye, Tess!" Saskia says. "Yes, you must try it on, Leila!" I know this means I'm not getting out of it. Whatever Saskia wants, Saskia gets. Saskia pulls me into a fitting room, dress in hand. She blocks the door and smiles.

"Just try it on," she purrs, inching closer to me. I gape at her. "God, you're such a prude! Fine. I'll close my eyes." She covers her eyes with her hands.

"I don't want to try this on with you in here." She keeps her hands over her eyes, and I angrily take off my pants and shirt, because it's just another battle I can't win. When I zip up the dress, I tell her she can look. When she does she look, it's with lust in her eyes.

"You're delicious," Saskia says, and my legs are jelly and my face is on fire. How can she still have this effect on me after everything she's done? "I love being in dressing rooms with you. Last time you were so nervous. Remember?"

"Can you get out now?" I plead, but she wraps her arms around my waist and pulls me close.

"We have time. Tess is still shopping."

"Why are you helping Tess, anyway?" I ask. Saskia leans in close and brushes her lips against mine. I momentarily forget where I am.

She grazes my cheek with hers when she whispers in my ear, "Tess is important to you. Or to your science grade, anyway. So I wanted to help."

I shove Saskia away. "What about Greg?"

She backs away slightly and rolls her eyes. "God, he's so dull. He only ever wants to have sex missionary-style. And he has very little stamina." She laughs a little but the whole thing is twisted, and now I feel a little sick to my stomach, thinking about the two of them together, thinking about poor Greg. I don't want to hear any more. As if I could stop her. "But you, Leila . . . You always have something interesting to say. You know about Hitchcock films, you pretend to like my jazz music, you even make me laugh, which not many people can do. Not a real laugh anyway." She inches closer again and grabs at my hips. In spite of myself, it feels good and a part of me wants to give in.

"But Greg's my friend," I whimper.

"Ugh!" she groans. "Fine!" She pulls her cell phone from her purse and begins typing a text message. "There."

"There what?"

"I broke up with him." She says this like she has just decided to make toast.

"*By text?*"

Saskia shows me the screen of her phone. It reads *It's*

Over. Sorry! Just like that. Like he didn't matter one iota to her. Like what he's feeling on receiving this message doesn't matter, either. She plops her phone back into her purse, then lunges forward aggressively and bites my lower lip.

"Stop!" I force her off me. She crashes into the wall behind her. I'm not sure what is happening, but she eyes me like a feral animal. Where are the store clerks to knock on the door? They're always available at the wrong times.

"Isn't this what you wanted?" Saskia asks in a sultry voice.

"Saskia, you hurt me." I look for any sort of sympathy in her expression. "Do you understand that?" Nothing. "I don't . . . This isn't what I want."

Saskia looks unmoved. "Then what do you want, you stupid dyke?" she asks icily.

Oh.

This bitch is *crazy.*

Saskia gets close to my face again and caresses my cheek. "No one is done with me until I am done with them. Do *you* understand?"

I'm getting a little scared now but don't let on. Saskia gives me an evil smile before she exits the dressing room.

As soon as I get my hands to stop shaking I change back into my regular clothes. I find Tess and Saskia at the cash register, paying for a dress Saskia has picked out. Tess is smiling, so at least something good has come out of this whole afternoon. Saskia signs her credit card receipt and behaves as though nothing strange has happened.

"Should we keep looking?" she asks Tess and me cheerily.

Tess looks worried. "Leila? Why are you shivering like that?" she asks. Instantly, Saskia's face changes. Her grin disappears and her eyes grow wide with fake concern. But I can't tell Tess what just happened without outing myself. Saskia knows it, too.

"Tess, can we go home? I don't feel well," I plead.

"But we have so many more stores to see!" Saskia says, throwing an arm around Tess like they are best buds. I have to get out of here.

"Please," I blubber. Tess rushes toward me and gives me a hug.

"Don't cry! If you feel that sick, I'll drive you home." Tess walks me out of the store and Saskia trails us, asking me what's wrong and why won't I tell my best friends what's troubling me.

TWENTY-SEVEN

I can't sleep. I keep analyzing every move, every sentence Saskia said in the changing room.

Then what do you want, you stupid dyke?

It was cold. It was brutal. I am scared of what she is capable of. I am terrified that she will tell someone about me and rob me of my privacy and my choice to tell or not tell my friends and family this fact of who I am. My anxiety grows as I imagine every scenario in which she could hurt me. She would just need to tell one person at school and the rumor would spread faster than Ashley's legs in Mr. Harris's science lab. Which is also a rumor that spread quickly. It would be only a matter of time before my parents would hear about their gay daughter. I imagine the parent phone chain coming to life. "Another snow day, right?" "No, Leila Azadi is a lesbian."

Stupid dyke.

I was stupid. Stupid to fall for someone so fast and for superficial reasons. She was gorgeous, she noticed me, she was charming . . . and I feel like the biggest sap on earth. Like the gumshoe in a film noir who lets the femme fatale pin him for the crime. "It was the broad, see! She's the one that done it."

What do you want?

I want to stop living in fear. I want to stop coming up with excuses about why I'm not interested in dating. I want my family to *know* me. I want to get to learn more about Lisa. I want to stop feeling like everything I am is inadequate or makes me unworthy of love because of something I can't help.

I know that I have to tell Mom. There's no getting away from it.

Morning finally arrives, and I've been up all night thinking about what I want to say. I keep thinking, too, about Kayvon and how his parents no longer speak of him. I wonder how long it will take for Mom to erase me from her memory.

I listen for the garage door to open to let me know Dad

is off to work. When I imagine coming out to Dad, all the bile and acid in my stomach lurch up to my throat. He gets upset and angry about mundane things like buying a rotten watermelon. When that happened, he went back to the grocery store and got in an argument with the manager for ten minutes, causing everyone in the store to stare as a brown man turned purple. Finally the whirring crank of the motor and clang of the chain let me know it's time to face my fate.

Mom is brewing coffee in the kitchen when I show up. "You're awake, Leila? But it's so early." I sit down on a stool by the kitchen island. I don't know how to begin this.

"Leila *joon*! You've been crying! What's the matter?" She hugs me and I just cry harder. Mom pats my head and makes comforting little cooing noises. I soak it in. I don't know if all this hugging and consoling will last when I tell her why I'm such a mess.

"You're going to hate me," I mutter into her chest.

"Is it your science grade? We can get you a tutor. It will be okay."

"No! It's not my science grade." I back away from her in frustration. She looks lost but also protective.

"What is it?" she asks. But this is too hard.

"You're going to hate me! You and Dad are going to hate me, so I don't want to tell you."

She inches forward and looks at me fiercely. "You're my daughter. I am never going to hate you. I might be angry with you, or disappointed, but I will love you until I don't have any breath left. You understand that?" At that last bit she chokes up, which makes me start crying again. Mom sits me down on the couch.

"So you'll love me no matter what?" I ask.

"Yes."

"I don't think you will."

"Try me."

How do people do this? How do people work up the courage to be themselves even if it means facing rejection from people who love them? Why don't people get medals for this?

"Your friends the Madanis, they used to have a son right?"

Mom frowns. "I wouldn't call them friends. More like acquaintances."

"Anyway, they had a son . . ."

"They still do. He's living in Phoenix near his aunt."

"But they kicked him out."

Mom is starting to catch on. "Yes. They did." The space between us is loaded with heaviness. I can't look at her face. I know what I'll see there. I will see her mouth tighten, I will see the frown lines by her lips deepen, I will see her eyes steel.

"No," my mom says firmly. "I didn't raise you to be that way."

I bury my face in my hands. I don't ever want to take my hands away.

"Stop. Stop crying. It's okay." I feel the weight of the sofa cushion shift as my mom stands up to walk away.

My nose is running. I wish Lisa were here with another tissue. What did I expect? That my mother was going to exclaim, "Finally! A lesbian daughter!" and lead me by the hand to the next Pride parade? I am a fool for doing this. I should have just kept it secret. Forever. How would my family ever know? I could just bring my "roommate" to Nowruz parties and distant cousins' weddings. Just friends, my "roommate" and I.

My mom puts her hands on my back and hands me a paper towel. I silently take it and wipe my face. She sits next to me again. She doesn't hold me or anything, but she's close. Close enough that's it's clear she knows she can't catch the gay.

"But you've never been with a boy before."

"No. I haven't." She's not advocating that I become the town slut and give all the boys at school a try, is she?

"Then how do you know? For sure?" How does she know she likes men? I could tell her that even though I've tried to like boys, I will never fall in love with one. I could tell her that I have wished my feelings away for months.

"I just know," I say. "It isn't going away." This time I meet her eyes. I need her to know it's serious, even if I'm embarrassed and ashamed. This matters, and I can't deny it.

"We're not going to tell your dad and sister," Mom says gently while rubbing my back. "Not now. Okay?" I nod and feel only relieved.

"Do you hate me?" I ask. Mom looks at me seriously and doesn't hesitate at all.

"I love you. You're my whole reason to exist. That's why this is hard."

What were supposed to be words of comfort make me feel like crap. But at least I don't have to pack my things and go. It could have been a lot worse.

"I need time," Mom says. "And maybe you will change your mind. You have your whole life ahead of you. But I know you've been keeping this from me, and you should never keep anything from me."

Maybe, but I don't think it's the right time to mention falling for a scarily unbalanced girl. I'm hoping I'll never have to bring it up. Mom tells me to wash my face and not to cry anymore. After I clean my face and look in the mirror, I text the first person who pops into my head. Really, she's been there throughout this whole conversation.

> Me: *I came out to my mom. There is snot everywhere.*
> It takes Lisa twenty seconds to text back.
> Lisa: *I'm so proud of you.*
> Me: *She doesn't hate me.*
> Lisa: *She never would. Your mom adores you.*
> I type and retype my next text at least five times.
> Me: *Is it weird that I text you now?*
> Lisa takes no time at all to respond.
> Lisa: *No. It's wonderful.*

Everything is heightened now that I've told my mom the truth. I've been observing her behavior for the past two days. I don't feel less loved or like she's ignoring me, but neither one of us mentions what I've said. She's praying a lot all of a sudden, I notice, which is weird because we're not religious. At night, before she goes to bed, she pulls out her prayer rug and faces east. It's funny, during the day she is this glamorous woman in tight sweaters and fitted pants. When she prays she's swimming in a sheet, with just her face showing. It makes her look so much older, especially when she bends her forehead to the floor. I think she's trying to pray that my lesbian inclinations will go away, but she never says anything about it, so I can't know for sure.

Dad doesn't even pay attention to my gloomy mood anymore. He just notices that I'm studying again, and that's all he cares about. I don't know when or if I'm ever going to tell him, but I'd better hope to God I get into medical school before he finds out. I still don't want to be a doctor, but I'm considering it now that I'm supergay and want to make it up to my parents.

When I come home from school the third day after talking to Mom, Dad is cooking dinner. He always gets excited and wants to show off his purchases when he has gone grocery shopping.

"Leila *joon*! Look, I'm making scallops! If you had this at a restaurant, one serving would cost almost the same as the whole pound that I bought today."

I wish I didn't love my dad so much and always want his approval. Maybe I don't try as hard as Nahal does because I already know I'm going to disappoint him. I figure I'd better just get some of the disappointment out of the way today. I'm on a roll.

"Dad, I'm not going to be a doctor." He stops cooking and looks at me.

"I know that, honey."

"You do?" I'm shocked. I mean, this whole time he's been telling me what a great job it is and encouraging me to take summer courses in biology.

He nods with a smile. "I know you've never been interested. But you can do whatever you want. Maybe not an actor . . . I don't know how stable that is . . ." He turns the flame on the stove higher and with a fork pokes at the scallops sizzling in the skillet. "I just want you to be happy. That doesn't mean you can get bad grades, though!" Before I can laugh, Mom walks into the kitchen.

"What are you two talking about?" she asks a little sharply. She wants to know if I've told him.

"Scallops," I say weakly. I don't know when I'm going to tell Dad my big secret, but I know he'll eventually figure it out. Maybe the same way he figured out I don't want to be a doctor. Maybe when I bring my roommate to Nahal's wedding.

After dinner and her prayers, Mom comes to my room to tell me good night. I'm in bed studying for my science quiz tomorrow. She smiles.

"I'm glad you're focusing on school."

"You mean instead of girls?" I shouldn't have said it, but we haven't talked about the big issue.

"Is there . . . someone . . . you like?" She can't even say "a girl." I don't want to tell her about Saskia being a psycho or how Lisa confounds me in the best way possible.

"It doesn't matter. Nothing could happen anyway, because you and Dad would freak out. I'm sorry I'm not perfect, like Nahal." Mom sits down next to me on my bed. I just lie on my side, looking at my book.

She takes my hand. "I was a very good student, you know. My parents didn't care that much. They focused more on relatives in Iran during the war in the eighties. I was fifteen when my family and I moved to this country. I kept doing well. I got good grades and I didn't go on dates. I was asked out a lot, especially by American men, handsome men. But it wasn't right. My parents wouldn't have liked it," Mom's never really talked about her dating history.

"I was getting my master's degree when I met your father. I had other Iranian suitors, too. But he was a nice man. He wanted children. My parents approved because he was doing his residency, and I liked him. So we got married. But I was so young and didn't know who I was yet. What I wanted."

"So you're saying you don't love Dad?"

"No, Leila. I do. But I always wonder *what if* about a lot of things. And I never want you or your sister to wonder *what if* about anything. Just because I didn't know who I was when I was young, doesn't mean you can't figure out who *you* are."

I think that's her admitting that she's okay with my liking girls, and decide to seize the moment.

"Lisa's been really great lately."

Mom's eyes widen a little, but she still holds my hand.

"She's very beautiful," Mom says. "I thought you were going to say you liked one of those shaved-head girls." I laugh. Mom has never looked more gorgeous to me.

"What are we going to do about Dad?" I ask.

"I'll worry about him. But I know he loves you no matter what."

"He overcooked the scallops."

Mom sighs. "He usually overcooks something." She kisses me on the cheek. As she leaves the room, I feel like things are going to be okay.

TWENTY-EIGHT

I get a B on my science quiz and I couldn't be more thrilled. Science isn't kicking me in the gut so hard these days, and Mr. Harris shows he notices by drawing a smiley face on my quiz.

"I got a B, Tess!" I proclaim as I catch up with her in the hallway, where she's exiting her AP physics class. She rips the quiz from my hands and gapes at it while walking.

"Holy crap! I *am* a genius," she says, and kisses the quiz. I grab for it and smooth out whatever wrinkles Tess may have caused.

"Thanks are in order, yes. I owe you," I say. She gets an impish look in her eye.

"Anything I ask for?"

"Is this going to be about that stupid dance again?" I ask, already knowing the answer. When Tess drove me home from the mall after the dressing room fiasco, I was adamant that I wanted *nothing* to do with the dance. I don't want to be anywhere near Saskia unless I have to be, like school. I've only seen her walking by a few times, and usually I can hide or walk in a different direction to avoid her.

"It's going to be fun! I think," Tess says. We walk into the library during our shared free period and head for our usual table. It's already taken. Greg sits writing on his laptop, engrossed in whatever he's working on. We still haven't spoken even though Saskia broke up with him. I miss him. I approach him. Feeling my presence, he looks up.

"Hey," I say.

"Hey," he says back. We're an articulate duo. Don't guys normally just punch each other and then make up? Can't we do that?

"I'm sorry about being weird." It's the best I can come up with. He processes this for a moment.

"Well, you never could help being weird," he says with a grin. I think I've got my friend back. Tess approaches us and sits across from Greg.

"Finally! You two were annoying me with all your teen angst." I pull out a chair and sit next to Greg.

"What are you guys up to?" Greg asks. If only I were prepared to tell him. Or even knew where to begin.

"I'm convincing Leila that we should all go to the dance," Tess whispers, and Greg and I both groan.

"Sorry, Tess, but I'm not really going to be in a Valentine's mood when February fourteenth rolls around," Greg says. I would love to tell him I know exactly how he feels. He turns to me. "You were right. That girl was erratic as fu—"

I interrupt him, not wanting to get into the details of Saskia's wicked ways. "I'm sorry you had to learn that from experience. She's just bad news."

"She text-message broke up with me! What kind of person does that? And she was always hot and cold. Like one minute she was super into me and the next she was bored and shut off."

"I know! She's so infuriating!" I add, unable to help myself. "And what's worse, she makes you feel like you're her best friend."

"And she knows she's hot, so I would totally feel like a million bucks that she wanted to be with me."

Tess slams her notebook on the table and glowers at both of us. We stop our complaining and give her our undivided attention.

"I'm sorry, but I have had it with you two," she says.

Whoa. She faces me. "You, Leila, have been weirdly secretive and mopey and I have no idea why, but it's bumming me out. You're supposed to be the fun one! And lately I feel like I have to be the one to get us to do stuff while all you want to do is study for biology. Which is bizarre. So snap out of it."

Tess turns toward Greg, and his eyes widen. "And *you* are Greg Crawford! Awesome guy, great student, amazing athlete, but you've been walking in Saskia's shadow like she has an invisible leash just for you!" She scowls and leans in, and Greg and I both tilt back in our seats. "This year I was lead in a play, I have excellent grades, I am *finally* a varsity athlete, and in a couple of weeks I won't have to wear my retainer anymore. So I am going to that dance with my friends. I want the corsage, I want the awkward slow dance, I want it all. Okay?"

Neither Greg nor I say anything for a moment. Neither do any of the other five people in the library who have just heard Tess's rant and are staring at us. Tess leans back and covers her mouth in what I think is slight embarrassment, but maybe she's just wiping away the spit that accompanied our reaming out. Greg is blushing, but he can't seem to take his eyes off Tess. He does like outspoken women. I do know that about him.

"So are you two sad sacks going to suck it up and come to the dance with me?" Greg nods, his mouth a little open.

"I owe you for all the science tutoring," I admit.

"Damn right you do," Tess says, but she's smiling, and it makes me chuckle. She looks Greg in the eye. "And *Zombie Killers Part II* is *not* the best in the franchise. That honor goes to the original *Zombie Killers*." She slaps her notebook, picks up her pen, and starts writing with what appears to be fierce concentration. She is done with us. Greg looks at me with raised eyebrows and still-big eyes. I like aggravated Tess. We should annoy her more often.

Tomas is running lines with the kids, and he's hard on them! I've taken the role of good cop in this scenario, since I think they are all so cute. Tomas, after every rehearsal, tells me not to condescend to them and to treat them like real thespians.

"Thurston!" Tomas barks from the seats in the audience. "Are you taking this role on wholeheartedly or would you rather we give it to someone else?"

Thurston stands onstage and barks right back. "I'm taking it seriously! As seriously as someone can take this dumb play!" It's not so bad. Well, okay, it's pretty bad, but let him try writing a half-hour play with a full homework schedule and loony-toon girls on the brain.

"Thurston," Tomas says, "while our rendition of Cinderella is no *Scarface*, we are trying to impact an audience with our sincerity and your adorable faces. We have a chance to really get people to feel! And you're not going to screw that up for me . . . I mean us." Thurston folds his arms and glares at Tomas.

"Maybe we should take a break?" I say, and I hear the kids breathe a sigh of relief. Tomas pinches the bridge of his nose and sighs.

"Fine. Take five, you heathens," he says. The kids start to leave the auditorium, only to run into Lisa, entering in her squash gear. The twelve-year-olds swarm Lisa, telling her they heard how great she did at the match last weekend. Lisa and I lock eyes, and her smile widens. My stomach begins an elaborate gymnastics routine.

"So when are you two going to make out already?" Tomas asks, and I look at him incredulously.

"We're not . . . She's not . . ."

"Well, she doesn't visit rehearsal to watch tweens recite their lines. And I'm handsome, but I don't think we'd mesh well." I glance over at Lisa, who is smiling at the kids. She's adorable.

"We wouldn't work," I mutter.

Tomas bonks me on the head. "If I had someone to get through high school with, all the other nonsense would be worth it." I know what he's talking about. Robert and some of the jocks have been particularly ruthless to Tomas lately, probably because the cool girls aren't that interested in him anymore and so aren't there to protect him. The novelty of a gay mascot has worn off.

"I'm not as strong as you are," I say, and he beams. I rarely compliment him, because he makes it so hard with his gloating afterward.

"Listen, high school is just a phase," he says as he directs his attention to Lisa.

"But we might as well make the best of it while we're in it."

"If I leave rehearsal early, are you going to be verbally abusive to the kids?" I ask seriously. I've never left the middle schoolers alone with him, and I am terrified of how many parents might call Mr. Kessler tomorrow.

Tomas pats me on the shoulder. "I'll go easy on them. Besides, we only have half an hour left. I'll make them do Oscar acceptance speeches." He sometimes has the kids pretend they've won an Academy Award as a self-esteem boost. There's a lot of thanking their parents and imaginary agents.

"Thank you," I tell him sincerely.

"Yeah, yeah," he says.

I pry Lisa from the sticky grip of half a dozen middle school admirers, and we leave Tomas and the kids to their awards ceremony.

"How's home?" Lisa asks as she walks me to the tennis court bleachers. It seems like it's become our "spot," though I wish we had a "spot" that was in a warmer climate.

"Fine. Mom's been really cool, but I think it's going to take her some time to adapt. Not going to be making out with anyone in front of her anytime soon."

Lisa climbs up a few rows as usual. She sits and extends her arm, offering me a seat. I leave the usual few inches between us. Lisa takes out a cigarette and scrunches up her face at my disapproving look.

"Tess is going nuts about this dance," I tell her as she smokes.

"I know. She talks about it at squash practice all the time."

"It's stupid. Dances." Lisa nods and flicks ash off her cigarette. "Are you going to go?" I ask.

Lisa laughs and shakes her head emphatically.

"Well, I have to go," I say. "Mostly because of Tess and

Greg. Plus, my mom expects me to go. I won't have a date, though. Unless someone wanted to ask me ..."

I look at Lisa with what I imagine are my huge, fearful Bambi eyes. She doesn't meet my gaze. She just stares out at the empty tennis court and drops her cigarette onto the bench below us, crushing it with her foot. I try to keep my mind busy through the silence. Is there chocolate-flavored gum yet? Did I remember to clear my browser history of lesbian folk music sites? I've been learning a lot about Ani DiFranco. I don't even like folk music, but I guess I'd better see what all the fuss is about if I am to join my people.

"I'm only just starting to feel better," Lisa finally whispers. "And I don't want you to have to pick me up when I break again." Her eyes begin to tear up a little. It's the first time I've seen her cry since we were kids. I put my hand on hers.

"When you're ready, so am I." She smiles through her tears and she rests her head on my shoulder while I rub her back.

"Do I have to say something cheesy from a movie now?" she asks through her tears.

I nod.

"You had me at hello."

I chuckle and so does she, in between her sobs.

TWENTY-NINE

The next few weeks are filled with soulful looks between Lisa and me; avoiding Saskia, who's seemingly taken up residence on Robert's lap; and shaping the talents of the middle school cast. At last it's the night of the Valentine's Dance. I'm putting on a dress Nahal helped me pick out. She sits on my bed, playing with her camera. Mom has made her official photographer of the evening.

"How do I look?" I ask her.

"Cute. Lisa will love it." I open my jaw and Nahal just grins.

"How did you—"

"You don't think Mom could process your lesbianism

alone, do you? She called me when you told her, and she's been keeping me up to date. I'm impressed."

"You didn't say anything!"

"It's not a big deal. I think it makes you interesting. Plus, it makes whatever guy I want to date look amazing! In fact, I don't think it stops there. I could get a tattoo on my face if I wanted and Mom and Dad wouldn't say a word. So, thanks." She grins while I pout.

"Seriously though, the ladies are lucky to have you," she says, and I give her a small smile.

"Thanks, Nahal."

We go downstairs, where my date is waiting for me with Taryn, Simone, and Christina. Dad looks him over with skeptical glances but engages him in conversation. I hope Dad's not scaring him or repeating the same story about that time I smeared yogurt all over my face when I was three and we had company for dinner. Dad smiles and tells me I look beautiful, then turns back to my date and gives him a stern look.

"Don't get my daughter into any trouble," he says, and Tomas looks a little scared.

"I doubt we will get into any trouble, sir."

Tomas pulls a plastic box with a corsage in it from behind his back. It's a white orchid dyed with rainbow colors. I laugh and give him a hug.

"Your dad is kind of intimidating but cute," Tomas whispers. "A short, balding bear."

"Does anyone want soda?" Mom asks as she directs her attention to the tech crew. They all look a little uncomfortable. Simone is clearly into the whole dance thing, as she's wearing a tiara and a puffy pink prom dress. Christina is stuffing her face with appetizers. Taryn is wearing a dress and combat boots. She doesn't really want to come, but for once she's being a sport. We're just waiting on one other couple. When the doorbell rings I answer.

Tess looks amazing. Her red dress looks even more beautiful on her than it did on the hanger. It accentuates her athletic frame, and it's nice to see her show off what she's working with. She's wearing makeup and her chestnut hair is piled loosely on her head, wavy and full. Greg is linked to her, beaming. They look really cute and happy together. I yell to the group behind me. "Okay! Photo time!"

As soon as we arrive at the dance, the tech girls take to the dance floor. Well, Simone takes to the dance floor and drags Taryn and Christina along with her. The cool kids aren't here yet. They usually show up drunk when the dance is about over, so we don't have to worry about them for a while. Tomas is complaining about the weak decorations to

Greg, who nods without bothering to check out the cheesy foil cupids and 3-D crepe-paper hearts that festoon the gym.

Tess drags Greg to the dance floor. I have to admit, he's a good date, putting up with all of Tess's notions of romance by slow dancing cheek to cheek when all the songs are fast.

"Nerd love," says Tomas. "Adorkable."

Speaking of nerd love, I notice our chaperones, Ms. Taylor and Mr. Harris, talking in the corner. Ms. Taylor looks less interested in Mr. Harris's obvious pleading than Greg is in the decor. Against my better judgment, I walk over.

"Hi, Ms. Taylor!"

Mr. Harris shuts his mouth.

"Hi, Leila! You look great!" she says, equally perky.

"So do you! That dress is just fabulous!"

When Mr. Harris walks away, we ditch the over-caffeinated act.

"Thanks, Leila. I was about to give in."

"He looked sincere, whatever it was he was selling."

"Men are stupid," Ms. Taylor says, and I chuckle. I'm always going to think of Ms. Taylor as one of my first big crushes, albeit a teacher crush, but now she's like a friend. She does look superhot, though.

"So, you here with anyone special?" she asks.

"No, just a friend. A guy friend."

"Well, that's nice. College will be different, Leila. Women will be lined up around the block. I had a phase in college actually . . ." I really want her to keep going with that story, but my attention is elsewhere.

She's here.

I say good-bye to Ms. Taylor and approach Lisa, who's looking stunning in a black halter dress. She doesn't look self-conscious or awkward, like a lot of the other girls in their updos and caked-on makeup, teetering on stilettos. She looks serene and natural, like she's used to wearing a beautiful dress.

"Hi." I'm glad the lights are dim since I can't tear my eyes away from her.

"You look . . . like you didn't dress yourself," Lisa replies.

"Can't you just say I look nice?"

"You look nice. More than nice, actually," she says, quirking a brow, and I feel like my smile is going to make my face explode.

"You're gorgeous. Don't you find it exhausting, being so pretty?" I ask. She laughs and takes my hand.

"Only as exhausting as keeping up with your train of thought sometimes."

"What made you decide to come?" I had wanted Lisa

to come with our group, even if she wasn't ready to be my date. She said she'd think about it but never gave me an answer, and I didn't expect her to show at all.

"Some girl," she says. "She's not so bad." I look down, suddenly shy, and realize we're still holding hands.

There's a shriek over at the snack table. The cool kids have arrived. Ashley is covering her mouth with her hands. She stares at Tess. They're both wearing the same dress. The dress Saskia picked out for Tess. Ashley looks like she's about to murder someone, and Tess takes cover behind Greg. Saskia walks up to Ashley.

"Oh dear! How embarrassing for you, Ashley." Saskia smirks and Ashley runs out of the gym, crying hysterically. So that's why Saskia wanted to go dress shopping with us. Robert stands behind Saskia, his eyes lidded and a hand on the small of her back, drunk and wobbling.

Saskia looks around the dance floor. When she sees me, she shrugs Robert off and makes her way over. Saskia looks at me, then at my hand in Lisa's. Her nostrils flare, and she has the sinister glint of a James Bond villainess in her eye.

"Hi, ladies. Lovely party, no?"

Lisa and I don't respond.

"Aw, that's sweet, Leila. A Muslim and a Jew. You guys should be on a poster for the United Nations."

I let go of Lisa's hand and face Saskia the way I should have weeks ago.

"Why don't you go take care of Robert?" I say. "He looks like hell."

"He'll be fine. It's you I'm worried about. Do you think it's really going to work with her? All she does is brood and smoke! She's hardly a conversationalist. Unless she's talking about her dead brother." I lunge at Saskia, shoving her back. The DJ has stopped the music and all eyes are on us. I feel Ms. Taylor put her hand on my shoulder. Saskia just laughs.

Mr. Harris is talking to Robert and clearly finds out that Robert is severely under the influence when he throws up all over Mr. Harris's shoes. I would enjoy the scene, if I weren't in the middle of a catfight.

"So you finally show some anger," says Saskia with a sneer. "It's about time. What are you going to do? Nuke me?"

"Girls! That's enough!" says Ms. Taylor.

"I'll say when it's enough," Saskia says. She leans into me, grabs my face with both hands, and plants a giant, wet kiss on my mouth. I struggle to get away, but she's holding me tight. When she lets me go, I fall backward a little and Lisa catches me. "Now you finally get what you wanted! You've been harassing me to kiss you for months, you predatory lesbian." Saskia throws her hands wide, laying it on thick for her audience. "There! Now everyone knows what you are!" It works. Everyone at the dance is entranced by the spectacle. The jig is up. My nightmare has come to life. I can only stand there, breathing heavily.

Greg and Tess are watching, mouths open. Tomas has his eyebrows raised and is clearly enjoying the intrigue. He probably wishes he were taking notes on the delivery and timing. Taryn, Christina, and Simone signal me with punching motions, suggesting that I beat Saskia up. I'm frozen and don't know what to do, until Lisa takes my hand in hers.

Standing by my side, she looks into my eyes. It's okay. It's all going to be okay. "Are you ready?" Lisa whispers. I think about all the worry, all the fear, all the anxiety over something that I can't help, that's beyond my control. I'm so very, very tired.

I nod.

Lisa kisses my temple and I hear a collective gasp.

"Yeah. Now they all know," I say. "Thanks." Lisa and I walk out of the gym to the thunder of hollers and applause.

Once we are in the hall, I feel like collapsing. Lisa rubs

my back. I can't believe I'm out. What if Dad finds out? What if he kicks me out? What if I lose my friends?

"Lisa, I'm sorry! You didn't have to . . . You can go back in. Tell everyone it's a misunderstanding."

Lisa just looks at me, but her eyes are filled with tenderness and patience. Once I start rambling I can't stop. "I just mean, you're important and beautiful and you don't have to feel like you have to—" I can't get anything else out because Lisa pushes her lips to mine.

The brave thing to do would have been to go back to school on Monday and face everyone after the dance, but honestly, I'm enjoying daytime TV too much. I've noticed that some of the women on *General Hospital* are superhot. I wouldn't mind being sick at their hospital, and my life is kind of a soap opera these days anyway—I might as well get pointers on how to get through it. So I've been faking sick for three days. I decided on a stomachache as my illness, since it's doesn't require a fever. Dad has been inspecting me, but they don't know I've been going to WebMD to make sure my symptoms remain accurate.

Lisa has called my cell phone a few times, but I can't talk to her.

The only one not buying my illness is my mom. She's

been attentive, but not so much to my physical ailments. Instead she keeps asking me if there's anything I want to talk about, but I shrug and say everything is fine—even though I've been in the same sweatpants and T-shirt since Monday. I haven't slept much, and my hair looks like the bride of Frankenstein's. Not symptoms of a stomachache. Also not the best time for anyone to come visit me, but Lisa does anyway.

"Leila, Lisa is here to see you" is all the warning I get. Lisa looks great, as always, and I keep wondering what the hell she would want with someone like me.

"I heard you were sick," she says with just a hint of an eye roll.

"Yeah. I'm not feeling so great," I mumble.

"I'll go get you girls some tea," Mom says, picking up on the tension between us, and heads to the kitchen.

"What are you doing?" Lisa asks.

"Watching *General Hospital*. You know, it's really not as bad as I thought it would be. There are a lot of plot intricacies, nuanced performances."

"That's not what I meant, Lei." Lisa puts a folder full of homework on my bedside table. I nod in appreciation.

"I was feeling like we were going to do this thing together?" she says.

This thing. This relationship? Are we going to sign our

parents up at PFLAG and wear matching T-shirts that say: I'M NOT A LESBIAN BUT MY GIRLFRIEND IS? We haven't even had time to figure "this thing" out. When Lisa dropped me off at home after the dance, we looked at each other like dewy-eyed baby seals. But we can't do that at school without some jerk smirking, thinking of us making out, I'm sure.

"I want to. It's going to be hard, though. My dad still doesn't know." Lisa sits down at the edge of my bed, far enough away that Mom won't think something "funny" has been going on when she gets back.

"I don't get why you'd want to do this," I continue. "I mean, you have everything. You could just date some guy, maybe Robert or someone in his group."

"He's suspended for drinking on school grounds. Plus, I'd probably have to drive him everywhere once he gets that inevitable DUI."

"Is Saskia still at school?" I ask.

"Why do you care about her?" Lisa says angrily.

"I don't care about her. She just . . . she—"

"Scares you."

"You don't get it," I say.

"I get that you're scared. You're scared of everything."

"I am not!"

Okay, maybe I am, but maybe I have reason to be.

What if my dad finds out and kicks me out of the house? What if he cuts me off financially? I'll be homeless, and who is going to take me in then? Ms. Taylor? She'll probably bore me with stories of her dates, and then tell me her apartment is getting too crowded, what with the appearance of her new man candy. Then I'll be on the street, selling balloon animals in Harvard Square, only I don't know how to make balloon animals, so they'll all be snakes or worms. The children I sell them to will be disappointed, the parents of those children will want their money back, and all the other street performers will laugh at me. Everyone will laugh at me.

What scares me the most, though, is the possibility that Lisa will figure out that I'm not good enough, and she'll leave me. And I'll have to do it alone. I don't think I could manage it.

"I'm not going to let anyone hurt you," Lisa says. "Saskia is suspended, and she might be expelled. And even if Saskia does rear her ugly head on campus, Ashley already has her sights on her for that dress thing. And your friends, if they really are your friends, won't care."

"How are people treating you?" I ask. I'm worried about Lisa, but I also want to know what to expect.

"I'm used to being talked about, Lei. It doesn't bother me. I don't really care about other people. I've only ever cared about you . . . and that scared me for a long time." She reaches across the bed and takes my hand. "If I can get over my fear, why can't you?"

I didn't think Lisa was afraid of anything. Even before her brother died, she was always quiet, but she took things head-on.

"I kind of can't believe you like me," I say. "I mean, I fart at inappropriate times, I never know what to do with my hair, I'm awkward . . . I just don't get it."

Lisa looks at our hands joined together. "You're also beautiful and kind, and you know me better than anyone else. Plus, everyone farts." Lisa gazes into my eyes. *Swoon.* "You need to stop questioning this. If you're not into me, just tell me."

"Of course I'm—I mean, I'd have to be crazy not to like you."

"And you think I'd have to be crazy to like you? That's kind of messed up, Lei. Where did your confidence go?"

I don't know. Lisa and I just stare at each other for a while, her hand still holding mine. That's when mom comes in with a tray of tea and chickpea sugar cookies. Lisa moves her hand away, but my mom catches it, and her eyes widen a little bit. I wait for her to kick Lisa out or start praying in the middle of the room, but instead she invites Lisa to stay for dinner. My mom is full of the best kind of surprises.

When Dad gets home, he's actually really excited to have Lisa over for dinner. He loves company. It gives him an opportunity to show off. He makes jokes and tells stories that the family has heard a billion times, but with guests it's usually only their fortieth. The stories and jokes are never all that funny, but the guests laugh right along with Dad. Tonight he reminisces about Lisa and me in elementary school, when we would complain and make fun of teachers we both kind of hated. Lisa is handling it all like a pro, while I'm just sweating, wondering if Dad is going to figure out that Lisa and I are Lady Gaga for each other. But he doesn't. He shovels down basmati rice and eggplant stew, which my mom whipped up on short notice, having remembered it's Lisa's favorite.

Mom kind of sneaks sideways glances at us throughout the meal. I can't really read her expression, but I guess she's still trying to get her head around this whole "my daughter is gay" thing. And now this "my daughter has a girlfriend" thing. Of course, Dad eventually has to kill the whole evening by bringing up college.

"So, Lisa, where do you want to go to school?" Dad asks. He's been asking me this since I was in fourth grade.

"I'm not sure. A Dartmouth scout talked to me last soccer season."

"Dartmouth! That's a good school! Leila should apply there."

I know Dad didn't go to college in this country, but even someone from Mars should know I don't have the grades to get into Dartmouth.

Dad goes on asking questions about Lisa's university prospects.

"So you're going to play football in college?"

He means soccer, but Lisa catches on.

"No. I probably won't have time. I want to be pre-med so—"

Dad slams his hand on the table, interrupting her, and smiles broadly.

"You see, Leila! One of your friends has sense! Lisa, can you please convince my daughter to follow in your footsteps?"

"I'm trying my best." Lisa grins, and I feel like kicking her under the table. Mom gulps more water than I have ever seen her drink in one go. "Actually, Leila's a really good director. The kids in her play adore her. I'm sure they've really missed her this week." Out of the corner of my eye, I see my mom smile.

"Well, I'm sure Leila is feeling a lot better by now,"

Mom says in a tone that clearly means: You're going to school tomorrow, kiddo. "Right, Leila?"

"If Leila feels up to it, would it be okay if I drive her to school?" Lisa asks.

I look down at my lap, afraid of the answer.

"I think that's a fine idea." Mom says, and I lift my head in time to see her smile warmly at Lisa. Mom then looks over at me, and I see all the love she's ever had for me and ever will in her eyes.

Maybe everything won't be so bad.

Maybe.

When it's time for Lisa to leave, I walk her to the door and she kisses me on the cheek. If my parents happened to see, they wouldn't really think it was weird, since we always kiss fellow Persians on the cheek when we say hello or good-bye. Lisa can be an honorary Persian, especially since she wants to be a doctor.

After Lisa leaves, Mom is waiting for me in my room. I finally tell her what happened at the dance, and that Dad should probably know I'm gay, because I don't want him to find out from someone else. She wipes a tear away before telling me she'll try to find the right time to tell him.

THIRTY

The ride to school the next day makes me anxious, but Lisa holds my hand the whole way, even when merging onto the highway, which is pretty impressive. She put on a mix of songs we used to listen to when we were younger. "Part of Your World" from *The Little Mermaid* comes on, and I yell, "Oh my God, you loved that movie!"

Both of us start singing along, each trying to outdo the other. Lisa has a decent singing voice, of course, because she's so perfect. I, on the other hand, squawk like that wise-cracking seagull in the movie.

Lisa grabs my hand tighter. "I guess I was a little gay from the beginning. I had a huge crush on Ariel."

"I didn't know that."

"We watched that movie, like, three times a day that one summer."

"Yeah, but I thought it was because of the story. She wanted legs, couldn't be with her love, that sort of thing. Plus, the sidekicks were funny."

"Well, I didn't really *know* I had a crush on Ariel. I just thought she was pretty. I thought the prince was pretty, too."

"So you're bi?"

"Can't some things just *be*? I'm a Leilabian for all I know." We pull into the school lot, and Lisa puts the car in park and turns to me, taking my other hand. "If anyone says anything to you today, just ignore them," she begins. "Or come find me. Some people are douche bags. But some people can be really great. Just focus on the really great ones, okay?"

I can't help but smile. "You're very cute, you know."

"Yeah, yeah," Lisa says, waving me off, but a little blush creeps up those pale cheeks of hers.

As Lisa and I walk into the school together, we're met with a lot of glances. There are boys grinning in our direction, giving us the thumbs-up in a perverted kind of way, and there are some younger kids that giggle and snicker. But when Ashley approaches us and gives them a sneer, they all flee.

"Hi, ladies. Did you screw before you got here?" she asks. At first I'm a little scared, but Lisa laughs.

"Wouldn't you like to know?" Lisa says, and Ashley grins back.

"Yuck. TMI. Listen, Leila, if you're going to hang out with us on occasion, we need to get you a sexier look. We can talk about it at lunch." Wow. She's even bitchy when she's trying to be nice.

In first period I sit next to Tess, who smiles and offers to give me her notes for the classes I've missed.

So that's why you've been so weird, Tess writes on her notebook and, as stealthily as she can, slides it in my line of vision.

Sorry I didn't tell you. I wasn't really planning on letting you know like that. I write back in my own notebook, edging it toward her and studying her face as she reads. She bites her lower lip, and I guess she's trying to think of the right thing to say. At least she's still talking to me. Or writing to me, anyway.

How are you feeling?

I feel anxious, a little scared, excited. *Free,* I write.

She takes in that last note for a moment and then smiles and scribbles. *So I could have gone after Greg this whole time?* ☺

I snort but remember where I am and quiet down. Tess slides her notebook back in front of herself and pats my shoulder before writing down the lecture verbatim.

After class I try to catch up with Greg. He's sitting in the computer lab and doesn't look up at me when I hover next to him. I wish he would acknowledge my existence, so I could try to get some words out. Nothing comes. When the bell rings he logs out of his e-mail and walks to class, pretending I was never there.

In science class Mr. Harris tells me I can have extra time for the paper that was due Monday. He's actually being really sweet; I guess he's not such a bad guy after all. I still don't understand anything in his class.

In Ms. Taylor's class Lisa and I sit next to each other. I can feel everyone staring at us. I wonder what they think is going to happen? That we're just going to make out on the desks and tongue wrestle through the lecture on Camus? Ms. Taylor notices all the stares.

"Guys? *The Stranger*? Any thoughts or are you all just going to keep staring at your classmates?"

Everyone gets embarrassed and goes back to the

reading. Ms. Taylor gives me a wink. Lisa writes me a note. *Are you okay?* I write her back. *I think so.* I also draw a smiley face. When I get a note back, she's drawn a heart.

At play rehearsal the kids are all excited to see me back and I'm excited to see them. They tell me Tomas was a terror while I was gone, but I can tell they still adore him. A few of the kids ask if Lisa will be at more rehearsals since we're girlfriends. I don't know if that's what we really are, but it's looking that way, and boy, word travels at light speed if it's gotten to the middle school already.

We run through a few scenes and remind the kids that dress rehearsal is next week. After rehearsal Tomas and I walk out of the auditorium together.

"God, you and Lisa are so sickeningly cute, Tomas says. "I'm jealous."

"Yeah we are." I grin.

When I get into Lisa's car at the end of the day I take her hand and hold it firmly all the way home.

THIRTY-ONE

My mom and dad haven't been talking to each other for a few days, and I know it's because of me. They're both trying to hide it, but dinner is a dead giveaway. Mom doesn't say anything and just pretends that everything's okay, even though she and Dad are not communicating. Dad is being sweet to me, but it looks like something's on his mind, and it has to be because Mom told him about me.

Everything in the house feels very fragile. I'm certain I'm going to be the first thing to break, so I call the only person who knows them as well as I do.

I call her on my cell phone in the bathroom, sitting on the toilet with the lid down. "I think Mom told Dad about me," I whisper. "They're being really weird. They aren't talking to each other, but are trying to be all friendly around me."

"Really?" Nahal asks.

"Yeah. It's weird. Dad especially. You'd think he wouldn't be talking to *me* instead of shutting Mom out."

"I guess he's shooting the messenger. Or maybe he doesn't believe her."

"I feel awful. If they divorce because of me, you can totally hate me forever."

"Stop being so dramatic, Leila. He's probably just working it all out. It's a lot for them, being from the *old* country," Nahal says with sarcasm in her voice. "I think it's a good sign he's still talking to you, though. He's not treating you any different. Besides, would he want to talk to you about boys, either? It weirds him out, talking to us like we may actually have love lives." That's true. I guess that's why Nahal doesn't bring around anyone she dates unless it's serious.

"Can I come live with you if they kick me out?" I ask. I can't tell if I'm joking or serious.

Nahal just sighs. "They both love you like crazy. Don't worry." I spot an ant walking across the tile floor of the bathroom and I think, *You lucky so-and-so. I bet you don't have these sorts of issues at your colony.* "Leila?" Nahal asks. "You still there?"

Barely. "Yeah. I'm here." We both don't say anything for a while. We've never really done this sort of *comforting* each other before. It's nice but it's strange.

"You looking forward to Farzaneh's wedding?" Nahal asks. It's this weekend. I had completely forgotten about it.

"No. I'm not." Since we're in the spirit of honesty.

"Can you believe the bridesmaid dresses are beige? Gross. Sepideh is going to look so bad. I can't wait!" Nahal makes a barfing noise, and I'm really glad she's my sister, something I never thought I'd feel in a million years.

Some days our ride to school is the only real time Lisa and I have together. Ms. Taylor is running a tight ship lately, and until things stop being so weird at home, it seems best if Lisa doesn't come to the house. This weekend I have the wedding and she has a squash tournament.

"Greg's still avoiding me," I say on Friday as she pulls away from the curb in front of my house.

"I'm sorry."

"I just don't get it. He's my friend. Or I thought he was." I look out the window as we drive down the side streets. There's fresh snow on the trees. Lisa reaches for my hand and laces our fingers together. I turn and look at Lisa, who still pays attention to the road and drives slower than your average teenager.

"Does your mom know?" I ask. She continues to focus on the road, not even batting an eye, but she nods. "So how is she treating you?"

"She said men are pigs and my father is a great example of that, so she understands why I am experimenting." Lisa shakes her head and I flash back to moments when Lisa's parents would argue when driving us to soccer camp. They never yelled, but each criticized almost everything the other person did. I slowly take my hand away.

"Are you 'experimenting'?" I ask. Lisa doesn't answer but instead turns on her blinker and pulls over to the side of the road. The cars behind us honk as they pass, which makes her flinch. She puts the car in park and turns to look at me.

"That girl really messed with your head, didn't she?" I'm so happy Lisa doesn't utter her name. Thinking about Saskia makes me sick. Lisa pushes a strand of my hair behind my ear and holds my cheek with her palm. "You're not a phase, Leila. If anything, you're the only thing in my life that makes sense these days." I feel all the breath escape my chest. "I don't tell you that because I don't want to pressure you or scare you off. You make me happy, but I don't want to rely on you solely for that happiness. Hence, I save the feelings and sharing for my oh-so-invasive therapist." She kisses me lightly on my cheek and lingers there as if to say, *Believe me. Trust me.* When she lets go, she raises her eyebrows and looks me in the eye.

"I'm not a phase," I whisper, and Lisa nods.

"If you need me to be gushy, I can be. It's just not what I'm used to. But if you need me to reassure you that you're my love nugget, or whatever the hell it is people say these days, I can try." Lisa's brown eyes don't waver at all, and my heart is pounding so hard it might burst out of my chest.

"Love nugget, huh?" I say as I watch Lisa concentrate on the road again and put the car into drive.

"As long as we never serenade one another and scare off people with our horrible singing, I think we'll be okay," my girlfriend says as she looks over her shoulder to merge onto the road. Of course we haven't had the official "girlfriend" talk, but after that little display, I think it's safe to say the girl is mine.

"Want to make out after school in your car?" I ask,

finally taking some kind of ownership of my desires, and Lisa beams at me.

"Duh."

"He just needs time," Tess says of her new chum when I complain to her about the distance between Greg and me. Tess used to be the one asking *me* about Greg. I can't believe the tables have turned like this. "He's, I don't know, angry you didn't tell him." What am I supposed to do? Apologize for being outted by his ex? Tess and I walk down a crowded hallway, dodging the students calling out to their friends and rushing to their next classes. I have a free period now and Tess doesn't.

"Yeah, well, when you do speak to him, can you tell him none of this is about *him* and his ego. I need my friend back." Tess splits off to get to class, and I walk to a place where I know I won't be judged.

In the tech loft, Simone is knitting what I think is a tea cozy while Taryn lounges on a couch. Christina, sketching in her notebook, looks up at me as I enter. "Hey," she says. She shows me what she's been drawing. It's the castle for the middle school play. "It's going to be a giant backdrop painting behind your kids." I gawk at the design. I had no idea

Christina was so talented. She grins happily and pretends to dust her shoulder off.

I drop next to Taryn on the couch. She puts her arm around my shoulders and I lean my head on her shoulder in return.

"Would you be interested in signing up for the Day of Silence?" Simone asks, eyes still focused on her tea cozy.

"What is that?" I ask. Taryn takes her phone from her pocket and looks up the website. She hands me her phone, where I read that it's a day for students to protest the harassment of LGBT people and their allies.

"I'm trying to get a bunch of signatures for support before we ask the headmaster if we can do it," Simone explains. "I think it will be kind of cool."

"Sign me up," I say, exhausted. Taryn squeezes my shoulders and gives me a noogie.

THIRTY-TWO

"There is no LeBron James without Dwyane Wade. Without Wade, he would never have won a championship."

I can't believe I have to be at this table with the basket-ball brothers. There is no bigger or brighter function among Persians than a wedding, and Farzaneh's is turning out to be so opulent it borders on ostentatious. The hotel ballroom is packed with at least thirty tables, filled with mostly Persian people. There are a couple of tables filled with *khareeji*, or foreign, friends.

My parents are sitting at a table on the other side of the ballroom, close to the bride and groom. Farzaneh smiles when people start clinking their glasses for the couple to kiss. She kisses her husband at the long table in the front of the ballroom. The female guests let out a series of high-pitched yells. Us young'uns are in the back, waiting for this whole thing to be over. I stare at the large centerpiece made of white roses and white lilies, wondering if I should buy Lisa flowers. Would she think that's too cheesy? Is it too soon for that kind of thing? I wish there were a teenage lesbian dating manual.

"She's coming over here," Nahal whispers to me as Sepideh drags her boyfriend, Shahram, by the hand, beelining it for Nahal. Sepideh is wearing a beige asymmetrical bridesmaid dress that accentuates her figure but makes her look older.

"Aren't weddings the best?" Sepideh asks. Her boyfriend, however, looks like he'd rather be having a colonoscopy.

"It's such a beautiful wedding, Sepideh," Nahal says sincerely. It is. Fancy chandeliers, excellent mood lighting, and open-bar beautiful.

"I can't wait for my wedding someday," Sepideh says, batting her eyes at her sheepish boyfriend. "There are some guys here, Nahal, if you want me to introduce you," she offers in faux friendliness.

"Actually I'm seeing someone," Nahal says, and I stare at her wide-eyed. She's must be lying to one-up Sepideh.

"Oh? Did you meet him at Harvard?" Sepideh asks,

tucking all this information into her big hair to save for later gossip with her mother.

"No, at a party in Cambridge," Nahal says. "He's sweet." Maybe she isn't lying!

"What does he do?" Sepideh asks, and her boyfriend winces and tries to twist his hand away as she squeezes it even tighter.

"He's a puppeteer. He works at kids' birthday parties, schools—that kind of thing." Dad would have a heart attack. I think Sepideh is having one right now, because this is really not their dynamic. She has no idea how to respond to this curveball.

"That's so . . . nice," she manages.

Nahal fishes her phone out of her purse and finds a photo to show Sepideh. "His name's Jeff." Sepideh takes in the pixels and her fake smile falters. She passes the phone back to Nahal.

"Can I see?" I ask, and Nahal hands me her phone. Jeff looks like he's around Nahal's age, disheveled in a T-shirt with paint splattered on it. He's rugged and a little pudgy but cute, and he's carrying a laughing Nahal in his arms. It's weird, but they look really good together, like they fit.

"Your parents must be so thrilled," Sepideh drawls out in a syrupy voice that seems to put Shahram on high alert.

"I haven't introduced him to Dad yet, since he doesn't have his PhD in puppetry," Nahal jokes. "But Mom's met him and thinks he's a doll." Huh. You think you know a person. I feel my face contort into what I'm pretty sure is a smile.

Thankfully, the band starts playing Persian music, and all the guests rush the dance floor, Sepideh included, dragging Shahram behind her. The men outstretch their arms while quickly moving their feet, as though they are about to be met with a hug. The women sway their hips back and forth in time with the percussion and shimmy their shoulders flirtatiously.

"So, Jeff?" I ask Nahal, cocking an eyebrow.

Nahal shrugs. "I figured you had enough going on at home. But if you ever want to double-date?"

The bride and groom are now dancing in the center of the floor, and the clapping guests surround them. Mom and Dad are among them. I don't know if it's the beat of the music, or that Dad is with his people, speaking Farsi and reminiscing about the old days, but he's always happiest at these things.

Mom and Dad have begun speaking again, but Dad has been retreating to the guest room after dinner. I don't know if he's tired or if he just doesn't want to confront the giant, hairy Mr. Snuffleupagus in the room.

When the song finishes, Dad walks over to our table. "Girls, come dance!"

Nahal rolls her eyes but doesn't have the patience to argue and moseys over to Mom on the dance floor. Dad takes Nahal's seat next to me.

"Isn't this great, Leila?" he asks, and I nod. Together we watch the bride and groom dancing as the MC on stage says, "*Khanoum ha raghs, Agayoon dast,*" or "Ladies dance, gentlemen applaud." The men clap alone while the women continue to move their arms in fluid waves. "Don't you want this, too, Leila? A nice big wedding? A nice husband?" Now he stares at me with his hopeful, wide eyes. My shoulders crumple, and I can't look at him.

He knows.

Dad looks at Parsa and Arsalan, who are so bored they might fall asleep at the table. "What's wrong with you guys? Why don't you ask my beautiful daughter to dance?" Dad asks jovially, and the boys laugh politely. I slump lower in my seat and want to slide under the table and hide.

I want to believe my dad thinks I am beautiful, but I know my having a girlfriend must make me ugly in his eyes.

"I don't feel much like dancing," I say. Dad looks at me with a sad pout, and I feel like a failure.

"Are you sure?" he asks nervously. He's not talking

about dancing any longer. It really pains me to see him on the brink of heartbreak like this. I could lie and maybe spare his feelings. I could tell him the truth and try to prove to him that I'm just as good a person as I was before he found out I was gay. And I'm happier. And I'm doing better at science.

But I don't say anything. I don't answer him, and he quietly walks away from the table, leaving me with the basketball brothers, who resume debating LeBron's defensive skills while I do my best not to cry.

I wake up to the sound of Cat Power's "Silver Stallion," which is my ringtone for Saskia. It is 3:20 a.m., and we only got home from the wedding around 1:00 a.m. I hit "ignore."

She calls again. I hit ignore.

She calls me once more and I turn off my phone.

When I wake up for real in the morning, I turn on my phone again. I have fifty-six text messages and thirty-two missed calls from Saskia.

At first the text messages are sweet. Sickeningly so.

Hey gorgeous! Don't be mad at me, I just got jealous. Forgive me? Xo

I miss you!

I wish you were here with me.

Then she talks about her life, like I care.

My family is moving again. I thought you would want to know.

I came, I saw, I got bored, and it's time to move on.

For what it's worth, you made the year interesting. So thank you.

Then the messages are about sex.

Robert is a terrible lover.

I know I'm a better kisser than your sad sack girlfriend.

I bet you haven't slept with her yet. You know I'd be better.

And then the messages just get vicious.

Why aren't you answering, you stupid dyke?

I never even liked you. I just liked how pathetic you were and that you followed me around.

I was being charitable letting your disgusting tongue in my mouth.

Your ugly girlfriend is going to grow tired of you just like I did.

I don't read any more of them. I drop the phone to the floor and rush to the toilet, crouch above it, and dry heave.

I let Lisa talk about the squash tournament on our drive to school because I don't want to talk about my own weekend of disappointing my dad and being abused by text.

I observe Lisa as she speaks, studying how long her eyelashes are, how her mouth naturally curves downward, making her look like she's always about to frown.

"How do you do it?" I ask, and Lisa briefly glances at me, not wanting to lose sight of the road. "How are you so . . . brave?" And why is she with someone who is so afraid of everything?

"Xanax," she says, and I almost believe her until she sticks her tongue out. "I don't know. Being alone and smoking wasn't really helping much." I think of my Sunday spent cowering in a bathroom, trying to expel thoughts of a horrible girl by vomiting her away. "And I'm not that brave. I haven't visited Steve's grave since the funeral a year and a half ago."

"When you go, if you do, I'd like to go with you," I say as Lisa pulls onto the Armstead campus. She takes her eyes off the road long enough to snap her head in my direction. "If you want." Lisa turns her attention back to driving and parks her car in the junior lot. She unbuckles her seat belt and kisses me, hard and urgently, like I have just asked her to marry me. For a moment I feel lighter, and the pain of the weekend melts away.

• • •

I knock on the office that Ms. Taylor shares with two other English teachers. I've checked all schedules to make sure her colleagues are teaching.

Ms. Taylor looks up from her laptop and starts to smile, until she sees that I am crying. "Leila? What's wrong?" she asks. She stands up from her chair and pulls me into a hug. Every student should have a Ms. Taylor. I wipe away my tears and try to breathe deeply and compose myself. Ms. Taylor sits me down in her office chair and locks the door. She sits in the visitor's chair in front of me and offers me a box of tissues.

I cradle my face in my hands for a few minutes while she asks what she can do for me. I can hear in her voice that she really means it. I take my cell phone out of my pocket and find the text messages. I slide it over to Ms. Taylor and watch her read the texts, her expression going from confused to embarrassed and finally to bewildered. I've stopped crying, but breathing is still something I have to remind myself to do.

"Do your parents know about this?" Ms. Taylor asks, and I shake my head. Dad doesn't want to know I'm gay; I don't want him to think I have terrible taste in girls to boot. "She's been expelled because of what happened at the dance. I was in the headmaster's office with her parents, and they seemed at a loss as to what to do with her. She's had . . . problems at other schools." Well, at least it's a comfort to know I am not her only victim.

"This year has been . . . a lot, and I really feel like I'm . . . like I don't want to feel guilty or worried about who I am anymore. And I don't know how to do that."

"You don't have to be anyone but yourself," Ms. Taylor says. I *want* to believe that. I *should* believe that. "I'm going to make an appointment with the school counselor for you. Do you think you could do that for me? Go see her?" I'm not so sure about counseling. I don't think I'm depressed or crazy. Then I think of Lisa, who seems to be getting better and happier every day. She's in therapy. If she hadn't gone to therapy, maybe we wouldn't be together now.

"I'll try anything. Really." Ms. Taylor nods and dials an extension on her phone. She makes an appointment for me with Ms. Patel. While Ms. Taylor is on the phone, I look at the photographs on her desk. There's a small photo of her and Mr. Harris wearing lobster bibs at some outdoor pier. I guess lots of people have a hard time letting go.

THIRTY-THREE

The night of the middle school play is at last upon us. We're performing before the freshman play as a doubleheader. The kids are all pretty nervous. Tomas has rounded them up for a pep talk before the audience takes their seats.

"This is not just some trivial middle-school farce. This is drama, people. Theater! You are embarking on a journey that may one day lead to the bright lights of Broadway, or Hollywood, or public speaking at some convention. It's evenings like this one that separate the true performers from the rabble." I am glad he left his whistle at home.

"I think what Tomas wants to say is, we're both so very proud of you. You've spent a lot of time working together and listening to us when it wasn't always easy." I notice Thurston glaring at Tomas. "We know how hard you worked, *you* know how hard you worked, so let's show them what you're made of!"

"Yeah! Let's kick some ass!" Thurston yells, and his seventh- and eighth-grade friends cheer.

Tomas stays backstage to make sure the kids all have their costumes and props. I'm in charge of lighting and music cues in the tech booth. But first I open the auditorium doors with Mr. Kessler, and we hand out programs to our audience, mostly parents, because, well, it's middle school drama and not Eugene O'Neill. It's nice seeing some teachers and older siblings take interest, too.

Ms. Taylor shows up accompanied by a tall, handsome guy who definitely doesn't teach at Armstead.

"Hi, superstar," Ms. Taylor says as she gives me a hug. "I brought my friend Sanjay."

He shakes my hand and smiles. "It's nice to meet you, Leila. I've heard all about you." He's a stand up guy to come sit through a middle school play for a date.

"Good luck," Ms. Taylor says. Sanjay takes her hand as she leads him to a frontrow seat. It's almost time for the curtain, so I give the rest of the programs to Mr. Kessler. I rush up to the tech booth, where Christina is already inside, amped and ready to go, and put on my headset.

"How's it looking in this light?" Christina asks. I am beyond impressed with her handiwork. The backdrop on the stage looks like the inside of a ballroom.

"It's perfect," I tell her, and she smiles a toothy grin, complete with a lot of fang.

"I know! Taryn and Simone were freaking out in the back row a little while ago."

The house lights are still on as I wait for Tomas's signals that all are ready backstage. Mom, Dad, and Nahal walk in, and I can see them clearly from above. Nahal is wearing her eyebrow ring, which is kind of spectacular. I'm pretty sure she wouldn't be wearing it tonight if I hadn't come out.

I look back to my notes and make sure I have all the appropriate cues.

"Hey, look who showed up," Christina says, and I glance down at the auditorium doorway. Tess is holding Greg's hand and doesn't appear to be dragging him anywhere. I don't think he's here because he loves middle school theater, so maybe it's a start to, I don't know, rebuilding the bromance?

"It's time to play the music / It's time to light the lights." Tomas sings *The Muppet Show* theme. That means it's go time. I flicker the lights to let stragglers know that the show is about to begin. Mr. Kessler begins to shut the double doors when someone stops them and they swing open again. There is the loveliest girl in the world, clutching a pale pink rose in her hand. Lisa looks up at the booth and gives me a small wave.

I'm pretty sure I am in love with her. I should let her know after the show.

"Romeo?" Christina's nudge to my arm breaks me from my reverie. "It's showtime." I lower the lights and wait for the kids to take their places.

When they are all at their marks, I turn on cue one, which shines a single light on Libby in wing tips, an overcoat, and a fedora.

"This is the story of Cinderella," Libby says with perfect projection. At the beginning of rehearsals, Libby's lisp made her self-conscious and reluctant to speak up, but Tomas insisted on working with her, with surprising patience, until she owned the part of the narrator. "A story we all know by heart. She's poor, she overcomes obstacles with the help of magic, and she gets the prince. Well, that version is *borrring*." The audience laughs right on cue. "So this is our retelling."

The light hits the stage with Thurston in a dirty dress and messy blond wig, mopping the floor.

"Cinderella was an orphan," Libby says. "A cute, lovable, darling orphan." Thurston curtsies while batting his eyelashes.

Two seventh-grade girls enter dressed in blazers, their hair pulled back in ponytails. They are wearing pencil mustaches and biting on plastic pipes.

"Her only family was her snooty stepbrothers," Libby says as the two seventh graders, Stepbrother #1 and Stepbrother #2, stand on either side of Cinderella.

"Ah, what a fine day to be a man," says Stepbrother #1, and the audience laughs.

"Yes, it is wonderful to be able to do as we please. Say, brother, I've heard there is going to be a ball with plenty of eligible bachelorettes. Shall we go?" Stepbrother #2 says, tugging on his blazer sleeves.

"Cinderella, who was taught to put her stepbrothers' needs before her own, was always curious why they could do as they pleased and she could not," Libby says.

Thurston stands up straight, brushes himself off, and speaks in a falsetto, made funnier because his voice is already cracking. "Do you think maybe I could go to the ball?" he asks, and the stepbrothers do their best country-club laugh with their heads thrown back.

"Ba ha ha. Oh, you silly girl, you know it's only for the well-to-do," Stepbrother #2 says, smoothing "his" ponytail to make sure not a hair is out of place.

"The ball is for a *select* few," Stepbrother #1 says with a chortle. "And men of a certain . . . character, at that." "He means *with money*," Libby stage-whispers.

"Well, we're off to the ball. Ta," says Stepbrother #1, tugging his lapels and pursing his lips. The stepbrothers exit, muttering about the help, and ham up their snob walk, backs rigid and backsides stuck out just a little. I dim the lights except for the one on Thurston and Libby.

"Cinderella was filled with rage," Libby says.

Thurston screams like he's the Hulk.

"Cinderella was filled with sorrow."

Thurston sobs hysterically.

"Cinderella was exhausted."

Thurston falls to the ground and fans himself.

"So many feelings. So many."

"Cinderella was visited by a kindly spirit," Libby says. I hit the cue for flashing colored lights. Molly, a tiny girl dressed in a mobster's suit with a pair of wings on her back, enters from stage right.

"Who are you?" Cinderella asks in wonderment.

"It was Cinderella's fairy godmother," Libby says while Cassie scratches her chin with her fingers, like Marlon Brando in *The Godfather*.

"I'm here to make you an offer you can't refuse," Godmother says to a stunned Cinderella. The audience chuckles. Good, there are plenty of *Godfather* fans in the house.

"The fairy godmother explained she could give Cinderella one wish," Libby says.

"As today is the day of my daughter's wedding," the fairy *Godfather* says.

"I can have any wish?" Thurston asks.

"Anything you like," the narrator says, and the fairy godmother nods.

The play continues with all the things the fairy godmother is willing to offer, giving every actor a moment in the spotlight. She offers the chance to be an Olympic gymnast and snaps her fingers. One of the stepbrothers does two backflips. The kids act out all the various opportunities that are offered to Cinderella, which she turns down one by one, from wealthy banker to president to pop star. Finally, after several skits, Thurston interrupts.

"You know what I want?" he asks. The stepbrothers, the fairy godmother, and the narrator together yell "WHAT?"

exasperated by all the fabulous possibilities Thurston has passed on.

"I'd like a friend."

"That can be arranged," the fairy godmother says, and points to a pumpkin near Thurston's feet. I cut the lights. When I bring them back up, the pumpkin has turned into Jennifer, an eighth-grade girl wearing a pumpkin costume.

"Wanna crash the ball together?" the pumpkin asks. Cinderella and the pumpkin hold hands and the lights go out.

I turn off the lights and wait for the cast to assemble onstage. As soon as they all line up, I turn on the lights and the audience applauds. My cast is beaming, holding hands and bowing like they're in the Royal Shakespeare Company.

When the ninth-grade performance of *The Lottery* is over, the middle school kids meet up with their parents in the lobby and receive their congratulations.

"Much better than *Glengarry Glen Ross*," Mr. Kessler says with a grin.

Tomas puffs out his chest. "We are artists."

Mr. Kessler hugs both of us and goes to talk with the ninth graders and their parents.

Tomas turns to me and extends his hand. "Madame director, it was a pleasure."

I shake his hand firmly while looking him in the eye. "It was, wasn't it?"

Tomas spots Thurston, who is now in jeans and a T-shirt, and goes to high-five him. They yell in each other's faces like they have just won the Super Bowl.

My family walks toward me and Dad gives me a hug. "Well, that certainly was . . . interesting," Dad says. "Are you indoctrinating kids with your liberal views?" The twinkle in his eye lets me know that he's joking, or trying to. At least he's not being as critical as I anticipated.

"These are for you, sweetheart," Mom says, handing me a huge bouquet of tulips with a card attached. Mom kisses my cheek; Nahal stands behind her and grins.

"Read the card later," Nahal says, and winks at me. I still can't get over that eyebrow ring.

"Thank you for coming. It means a lot."

"Of course, honey," Mom says. She gives me a big hug, almost crushing the flowers in my arms. I look over Mom's shoulder and see Tess, Greg, and Lisa standing together. Mom backs away to follow my line of vision. "Let's let Leila be with her friends. Is . . . are your friends driving you home?" We both know she means Lisa.

Dad doesn't know yet that Lisa's my girlfriend, which for now is fine by me. He's still adjusting to my being gay the best way he can, not talking about it, but also not condemning me or loving me less. It's a good a start.

"Yeah, I'm all set," I say, and Mom nods.

"Before you go, could you persuade your sister to take that thing off of her face?" Dad asks me with a grimace, which gets a big eye roll from Nahal.

"We'll see you at home," Nahal says before walking away with Mom in tow. Dad lingers for just a minute.

"I . . . well, I don't understand all the things you do, but I am proud of you. You know that, right?" he says, and he begins to get misty-eyed. I've never seen him cry! I smile and he takes a deep breath. "Okay, good. Don't get home too late." He gives me a hug before walking briskly out of the performance center. My traditional, Iranian, conservative father, a teddy bear in a suit.

I head with my flowers over to Greg, Tess, and Lisa. I hug Lisa and when we release she hands me my rose. I'm going to make a giant poster to hold up when I cheer for her at the squash match next weekend.

I look over at Greg. I don't know if he's still angry, but his being here is a good sign. He folds his arms in front of him and quirks an eyebrow. "So when are we hitting the strip club together?" he asks, and Tess punches him in the shoulder. Greg just laughs and looks at Tess adoringly then asks her, "Can you give Leila and me a second?"

Tess gives me a hug and Lisa kisses me on the cheek before they walk over to Tomas and the tech girls. Greg looks at me intently, his brow furrowed, like he wants to form words but is somehow unable to.

"I'm sorry I didn't tell you," I begin. "I wasn't really telling anyone, if it makes you feel better. I got figured out *plenty* of times by people who have better gaydar than I do, but I didn't mean to hurt you."

Greg stuffs his hands into his pockets and looks down at his shoes, like an adorable little boy. "Leila, listen. I'm sorry if I was a jerk. I didn't know. I didn't know—you and Saskia."

"It's okay. I didn't tell you, so how would you know?"

"I don't care if you like girls. I do, too, so now we have more to talk about."

"I've always had a huge crush on the actress in *Zombie Killers Part II*," I confess. "You know, before she gets decapitated." He looks impressed and then nods slowly, as though he's finally putting together all the pieces of our previous conversations about her.

"No more lies?" he asks,

I shake my head. "No more lies." It's such a relief to have no reason to deceive him anymore. I've missed him. We pound it out with our fists, and I look forward to the time when we'll talk in complete detail about how Megan Fox was the only redeeming thing about *Transformers*.

When I get into the passenger side of Lisa's car, I open the card that was attached to the flowers from my family. It reads in big, bold letters: *We Love You Unconditionally! Mom, Dad, and Nahal.* I show the card to Lisa and she starts to cry for me. After a few moments she takes deep breaths and wipes away her tears.

"I don't know where those sudden allergies came from," Lisa jokes. I kiss her on the cheek.

"Lots of pollen in the winter. Totally understandable."

Lisa laughs and starts the car. It sounds like horses neighing, carrying us off to a long overdue ball.

ACKNOWLEDGMENTS

I want to thank Chris Lynch for being the best mentor in the whole wide world, Elise Howard for making this book so much better than it originally was, Pat Lowery Collins for dealing with the *rough* rough drafts of this story, Eileen Lawrence (Mom), Emily Parliman, Judy Gitenstein for all her help and patience, Leigh Feldman, Jean Garnett, Kelly Bowen, Open Book Publicity, Debra Linn, Craig Popelars, Elisabeth Scharlatt and everyone at Algonquin Young Readers. Amy Hanson Downing, Robin Cruise, my family for loving me, all the indie booksellers and librarians that have supported me, authors who have been so wonderful to me: Amy Herrick, Hollis Seamon, Sarah Dessen, Malinda Lo, Jacqueline Woodson, E. M. Kokie, David Levithan, journalists and reviewers who have been so gracious, my friends, every teacher I've ever had, and you, dear reader. I hope this book finds you and lets you know that you have a story to tell, too. Much love.

Read on for a preview of Sara Farizan's
first novel, *If You Could Be Mine*

1

NASRIN PULLED MY HAIR when I told her I didn't want to play
with her dolls. I wanted to play football with the neighborhood boys. Even though sometimes they wouldn't let me because I was a girl, they couldn't deny my speed or the fact that
I scored a goal on the biggest kid in the yard. Nasrin pulled
my hair and said, "Sahar, you will play with me because you
belong to me. Only me." That was when I fell in love with her.

We were six. We didn't wear head scarves then. We were little girls, not "whores of Babylon," to be met by the scrutinizing
eye of any asshole with a beard. Nasrin has the longest, darkest
hair but it never gets tangled or neglected under her *roosari*
like mine does. I always think there's no point in making my
hair look decent if I have to cover it in school, but Nasrin is
always taming her locks—blow drying, using mousse, a flat

iron sometimes. No matter what she does to her hair, she will always be the most beautiful woman I have ever seen.

It's difficult, hiding my feelings for her. Tehran isn't exactly safe for two girls in love with each other. I wonder if people can tell I love her when I look at her — in the park, at the bazaar shopping for bras, everywhere. How can I not stare? Even at age six, I wanted to marry her. I told my mother when I came home after playing with Nasrin, who lived a few houses down from our apartment. Maman smiled and said I couldn't marry Nasrin because it was *haraam,* a sin, but we could always be best friends. Maman told me not to talk again about wanting to marry Nasrin, but it was all I thought about.

I thought about marrying her when we were ten and Nasrin cried that I got my period before she did. I thought about marrying Nasrin when she taught me how to put on eye-liner when we were both thirteen. I thought about marrying Nasrin when we finally kissed, on the mouth, like Julia Roberts and Richard Gere did in *Pretty Woman*. It's a stupid movie, but Nasrin always makes me watch it with her. We got the DVD from my older cousin, Ali. He's in university and knows everything cool but gets awful grades. I don't like that the movie is dubbed; the voices never match the actor's lips. And Julia Roberts has big lips. She could fit a whole *kabob barg* in her mouth if she wanted to. It was three months ago that Nasrin and I kissed. Even though I'm seventeen now, it made me feel like I was six again and she was pulling my hair.

We are always around each other, so I don't think anyone will suspect that Nasrin and I are in love. She worries, though, all the time. I tell her no one will know, that I will protect her, but when we kiss I can feel her tense. She keeps thinking about the two boys who were hung years ago in Mashhad. They were hung after being accused of raping a thirteen-year-old boy, but most people think the two were lovers who got caught. I remember the video of the hanging my cousin Ali downloaded for me. I don't know how Ali gets away with the things he does, and would never ask, either. When I saw the video, I wasn't scared, but I got angry. They were so young, just sixteen and eighteen, blindfolded, standing next to each other in the square with nooses around their necks. I felt my neck itch as they were slowly raised on cranes. Whatever crime they committed, I didn't want a part of it. I wanted to stop loving Nasrin, but how do you stop doing something you know you are supposed to do?

Nasrin keeps telling me, "We aren't gay, we are just in love." I've never even thought about being gay; all I know is I love Nasrin more than anyone. Nasrin always used to giggle with the neighborhood girls about boys, but I never joined in. Why should I care if Hassan grew a mustache that looked like a baby caterpillar? It wasn't going to change the fact that I am in love with my best friend. It wasn't going to make my *baba* stop crying, wishing that my *maman* didn't die all those years ago. It wasn't going to change the fact that I had to teach myself to cook meals, and my *khoresht*s will never be as good as Maman's, even though Baba says they are delicious. I miss her sometimes, but these days I just resent her for not being here.

I've gotten used to Baba's long periods of silence. Sometimes he won't speak for two days, but when he comes out of whatever trance he's in, he is in a good mood and pretends nothing happened. I'm no doctor, but I think he is depressed. I wish he would snap out of it.

Nasrin is in my room, painting her fingernails while I pretend to do my science homework. I've been studying a lot for the Concours, which determines which university you get to go to and in what field. About one and a half million students take the exam every year in June, and only 150,000 get accept-able scores. Your performance on the exam is all that matters. Your grade-point average is meaningless, which Nasrin always reminds me when I get a less than perfect score on an Islamic Studies quiz. It's September now and I already feel anxious. I want to go to Tehran University to study medicine, which is just about every student's dream, but I think I actually have a chance. Nasrin on the other hand . . .

"You're staring again," Nasrin says. She looks up from her nails and gives me a smile. I look down at my textbook and hope my face isn't red, like all the other times Nasrin catches me watching her.

"Don't you have homework?" I ask.

Nasrin just blows on her nails and rolls her eyes. "I'm not a genius like you, Sahar. I'm going to move to India and be a Bollywood actress." She stands up and goes into one of her Indian dance routines. Nasrin is an excellent dancer and gets a group of girls together from her school to practice. They usually have me film them while they dance Persian, Arabic, or whatever other dance routines they have been working on. My favorite was when they did the Ne-Yo dance. Black American singers sound better than anything, though I fear saying that in front of Nasrin because she loves her Persian pop so much.

If she spent as much time on her studies as she did her dancing, maybe we could end up at the same university, but I know that isn't going to happen. Now that we are getting older, we have only a few more years left like this together. Things will change. Nasrin will have a lot of suitors. The men will line up on her block. All of the well-to-do in Tehran will come to her family's house, dressed in their best suits.

The suitors will have tea with Nasrin's parents, and they will explain that they can provide her a good life with whatever important and boring job they have. Her parents will pick the best man for her, meaning the one with the most money. Nasrin comes from a good family, and they have money themselves, so she will marry the best that there is. I am not the best. I am an awkward girl with breasts so big that sometimes I feel I might tip over. I don't know when I am going to lose her, but it's going to happen, and I don't know if I will be able to handle it.

Nasrin finishes her dance, and her face falls when she sees mine.

"What's wrong, Sahar *joon*?" she says. She's always been able to read me, even when she doesn't want to.

"I wish we could stay in this room forever," I say. She grins.

"Wouldn't you miss fresh air? The sun on your face?"

"The morality police complaining that your head scarf isn't on properly?" I always go by the rules, but Nasrin couldn't care less. She's always pushing the boundaries, with most of her hair showing at all times and a little scarf flopped over the end of her ponytail. Nasrin sits down next to me and takes my hand.

"We can't live in here forever. There's never anything to eat in your room, anyway." We both laugh, and she plays with my hair.

"I want to marry you," I say, and Nasrin looks at me with a sad expression that makes me feel helpless and pathetic.

"I know you do, *azizam*. We've talked about this,"

"We could run away!" I beg of her. I'd go wherever she wanted.

"We would get as far as Karaj and then what? Sahar, be serious."

I'm not as well off as Nasrin's family, so I couldn't provide for her, or even buy her a bus ticket to Turkey. When I'm a rich doctor, I'll buy her all the things she has grown accustomed to. Maybe until then I'll just lock her up in a shack in a village so no man will ever have her. I'll have sheep guard her, bleating at whoever approaches. Knowing Nasrin, she will probably be choreographing dance numbers with the sheep and putting a video of it on the Web.

"I'll find a way for us to be together." I look her in the eye to let her know I mean it.

She bites her lower lip, as she's done since she was little, and gently pulls at my hair. "We're together now, Sahar. Let's not waste time on what can't be."

What can't be . . . Sometimes I get so angry I want to take off my *roosari* and run into the streets like a madwoman, my hair flying behind me, waiting for Nasrin to pull at it. I see how Ali is with his boyfriends—they're very sweet together, but they are always hiding. Ali is perpetually dating someone new, but he treats the men like they are toys that he is eventually going to grow tired of. Ali introduces his gentlemen to me as his boyfriends, but usually the boyfriends look nervous and laugh like Ali is crazy. They say they are in Ali's class, but I know Ali has never cared much about schoolwork, and I'm pretty sure Ali is planning on studying anatomy when they come over. He's an engineering major.

I haven't told Ali about Nasrin and me. Though Ali told

me he was gay, we never really discuss it. I remember Maman telling me not to talk about it. So I don't. Ali, though, he treats it like it isn't a big deal when he's with me, which I don't understand. In public everything is secret, of course. I don't even know where he finds his boyfriends. A part of me doesn't want to know. I don't want to know what would happen if Ali got caught. It would kill my aunt and uncle in Tabriz, who send Ali lots of money for his "school" when Ali lounges about, smoking *shisha* and playing backgammon. There are things I don't understand about Ali, but I like that he didn't look at me with sad eyes when my mother died. He treated me like he always had, nudging me with his hip and giving me a wink.

I think about telling Ali about Nasrin because it's getting so difficult not to talk about how I feel. I want to shout how much I love her to anyone who will listen, but sometimes I feel stupid even saying "I love you" to Nasrin. I know she loves me, but once in a while I can't believe she could feel that way about *me*. I think that she just might not want to hurt my feelings.

"Maybe when I get into university we can get an apartment," I say, and Nasrin raises one eyebrow. I know. It was a stupid idea.

"You think my parents are going to let me move out of their house? Before I'm married?"

"You'd be living with me. I would keep the boys away," I say with a grin. She leans in closer to me. Her perfume smells like jasmine and vanilla. She's so cruel. I could die from it. Her mouth is close to my ear, and I think she knows how deliciously evil she's being.

"If my parents knew what a devil you are, they'd lock me in Evin Prison for lust." She says it with levity and I smile, but it very well could be a reality. Though I can't imagine Nasrin's parents putting her in any danger. They have spoiled her since birth because she is the baby of the family, with two older brothers. Her parents have always been very sweet to me, but I worry they are nice to me so I will marry Dariush, Nasrin's oldest brother. A family like Nasrin's would typically seek out other wealthy families to marry into, but Dariush doesn't have many prospects. He was suicidal a few years ago over a girl who wouldn't marry him. The girl's father said Dariush wasn't good enough for her because he's a mechanic. Nasrin's parents, Mr. and Mrs. Mehdi, have not produced children who have met their expectations.

Mr. Mehdi is a prominent exporter of pistachios to foreign

countries and it is fair to say that he is nuts about nuts. His wife comes from oil money generated during the Shah's time, though they will never admit it. They were hoping their children would be captains of industry or cancer-curing doctors. But their children had everything handed to them — happy birthdays, nice clothes, and the latest toys — so they had no incentive to try at anything.

Cyrus, the middle one, is hoping to take over his father's business and isn't lazy, but he isn't very bright. Dariush is a free spirit, more interested in learning how to play Cat Stevens songs on his guitar than making a living. Nasrin's only goal in recent years has been to acquire as many shoes as possible.

To Mr. and Mrs. Mehdi, I am the dream child they always wanted and also the example they set for their children. I study hard, I take care of my father, I cook and clean. I'm polite when Nasrin is sometimes too cavalier. When they compare Nasrin and me it isn't fair, and sometimes I think Nasrin resents me for it. We don't ever discuss it. If they knew about the relationship Nasrin and I have, I don't know if they would be more disappointed with me or their own daughter.

I tuck a strand of hair behind Nasrin's ear. She smiles and kisses my nose. I hate when she does that. She knows I do, she's just being tough on me today for all of my wishful thinking. I wonder whether Nasrin would be open about us if we didn't live in Iran. She might be just as scared but for different reasons. She's always been the loud one, but she's scared of stupid things. Things like spiders, the dentist, or not having the latest jacket. She squeezes my hand when she's scared, and lately my hand feels like it is going through early arthritis.

I lean in and kiss Nasrin on her lips. She returns the kiss with urgency, and I definitely know that no man or woman can ever make me feel the way she does. If that makes me gay, so be it.

Sometimes when Nasrin and I kiss, Ayatollah Khomeini's and Ayatollah Khamenei's faces pop into my head. When I was little, I used to think they were the same person, because their names sound the same, they wear the same outfit — a cleric's robe and a turban — and both with long gray beards. Khomeini, now deceased, became the Supreme Leader after the revolution. I hadn't even been born then, but apparently Iran was a lot different. There was a king and girls could wear miniskirts, which is all Nasrin cares to know about that era because it sounds glamorous. In school, they teach us that

Khomeini brought justice and the will of God to the people and how much better the country is flourishing than under the Shah. I'm not sure how much I believe that.

The ayatollahs' photos are everywhere. At the shopping mall, in small businesses, restaurants, parks, on the autobahn . . . and when I kiss Nasrin I feel like they are watching me. I don't know if it's to give citizens a sense of pride or to scare us from questioning our government. I think Khomeini is my "Angry Grandpa," and Khamenei, the Supreme Leader of today, is my "Disappointed Grandpa." Whenever I think of Nasrin in public or at school, I feel their eyes on me. Angry Grandpa is the most judgmental. His brow is furrowed as if to say he knows exactly what I am: a degenerate.

Ayatollah Khomeini has been dead thirty years, but it's as though he never left. He's always mentioned in news broadcasts. Khamenei speaks of him with great reverence during his national addresses, and he's depicted as the father of the country. People typically hold their tongues if they don't agree with that sentiment. Those who don't . . . Well, it makes their life a lot harder. There's a national holiday to commemorate his death. Some people make the pilgrimage from far, far away to visit his tomb and get one free meal given to visitors that day. Most people in Tehran try to get out of town and go visit the Caspian Sea.

Nasrin puts her tongue in my mouth and it makes me forget about Angry Grandpa for a moment. Her fingers run through my tangled hair, and I kiss her neck, making sure I don't leave a mark. We're always so careful, and being that way is exhausting, but we don't know anything else. We hear a knock at the door, and the two of us jump away from each other.

"Yes?" I say in my best calm voice while Nasrin looks into one of her books for the first time all afternoon.

"Sahar *joon,* would you and Nasrin like some *chai*?" my father asks from the other side of the door. This is his way of asking for tea for himself, but it's sweet that he thinks to offer, even though we both know I'm the best at brewing it to a rich, dark color. He puts in too many leaves or not enough. Baba is a terrible cook but a good man.

"I'll come and make some, Baba!" Nasrin is packing up her purse. I hate when she leaves. It feels like a wrestler is squeezing my lungs. "Do you have to go?" I know the answer.

"I have to go home sometime. Don't worry. I might come back, *if* I feel like it," she says with a mischievous smile. I worry that one day she might not feel like coming back. It's the thing I fear most. More than prison, more than the police, more than Baba kicking me out, and more than not getting into medical school. If I lost Nasrin, I wouldn't know what to do with myself. She puts on her head scarf, loose and stylish like she has no respect for the law, and kisses me on the cheek.

"Why aren't you a man, Sahar?" she asks seriously. I shrug, and she turns to leave. I look in my mirror to make sure my cheeks aren't too flushed before I go to serve Baba dinner. He never notices, but one can never be too careful. I'm always careful.

In the kitchen Baba sits at the table and watches me with a vacant expression as I put the kettle on and fill a plate with leftovers. I put the food in the oven and sit in front of Baba, waiting for everything to heat up. He smiles at me, but it's always the same sad expression. I remind him of Maman, and his heart breaks over and over and over. He says that I have the same big, expressive eyes that Maman had.

"When did you get so big, Sahar?" Baba asks quietly.

I want to say, "While you were sleeping through life," but I don't. My father is a carpenter and works on construction sites, mostly making furniture. When Maman was alive, he made the most beautiful pieces. Hope chests for a bride on her wedding day, chairs and tables that the well-to-do would commission. His pieces always have some imperfection now.

"I'm not so big, Baba. You're still taller than I am."

Baba smiles and runs his hand through his gray hair. He got old so fast. Mr. Mehdi looks like he hasn't aged since Nasrin and I were little, but Baba looks like he could be my grandfather.

"You're studying very hard?" He knows I am. It's just that we don't have much else to talk about.

"Yes. I wish the test would just come already so I would know my future," I say, already nervous about the math portion that waits for me in June.

His knowing look makes me suddenly shy. "No one knows the future," Baba says. "Anyone who thinks they do is mistaken. Remember that, my love."

We sit in silence for a minute before I decide to set the table. Sometimes I feel like I should set a place for Maman, because her presence is everywhere.

I feel guilty that I wish it wasn't.